F*CK YOU, YOUR HONOR

F*CK YOU, YOUR HONOR

By Craig Chambers

Black Letter Editions
Littleton, Colorado

Credits:

Book design by www.cedricchambers.com

Cover art by Cedric Chambers

Edited by Jami Carpenter @ www.redpengirl.com

With special acknowledgement to Michael Bozek

Gavel Icon made by Freepik from www.flaticon.com

Visit http://www.craigchambersbooks.com for more information and to subscribe to author newsletter

Printed in the United States of America

ISBN: 978-0-692-83159-5 (print)

ISBN: 978-0-692-83160-1 (digital)

For Reyna

1

When The Honorable Judge Solomon of the Algonquin County District Court sentenced me to write a book, I sat up in my chair at the Defendant's table and listened. This ruling was an extraordinary sanction. An unusual punishment I didn't deserve. I'd heard of fines, community service, probation, and jail time as punishment in court cases, never an order to write a book.

"Counselor," Judge Solomon scowled, "this book project is due in exactly one year. There will be no excuses, and no continuances will be granted. Not just any book. A book about the dignity and integrity of the legal system. At least sixty-five thousand words. Any questions?"

Could he do that?

That was my first question. I didn't ask it then. In the crowded courtroom — hot and stuffy, silent and small. I had learned to be deferential in front of a judge. A judge is a man of great power and insight. If I didn't follow the court's order, I could be disbarred. It was a privilege to practice law, and I didn't want to lose that privilege. I had bills and alimony to pay. I was an attorney, after all; I had no marketable skills.

Call the lieutenant governor, the deputy mayor! This was some kind of mistake!

I had been a lawyer for fifteen years. I had never been in trouble. I was the one who followed the rules, always returned phone calls, scoured my court filings for typos, never missed deadlines. I filed my pleadings at least a day early. I had been on television, and I had won a big case against Superman.

Maybe I hadn't heard the judge correctly. It was late July, the air conditioning in the courtroom didn't quite work, and the bailiff had brought in a rattling old fan. At the very least, I waited for an explanation of his reasoning. I waited for the word "but."

But the judge did not say the word.

I looked up at him perched in front of the courtroom behind the wood paneling in his flowing black robe, next to the empty seats in the jury box and the witness stand, the fan noisily limping along. The state flag and seal hung behind the bench. I saw the glaring red numbers of the digital clock, the big calendar on the wall of the courtroom.

I knew very little about this judge, except that he had been on the bench for a long time. Although he was a man of extraordinary authority, there was nothing striking about him. He had bad teeth; you would think with such a nice salary he could have them repaired.

If we could settle the dispute the old way, with a boxing match or a duel, for example, I would clearly have won.

I noticed the bailiff, the court reporter, and the sheriff. The crowd of disgruntled homeowners appearing in court for the first time, trying to keep their homes out of foreclosure.

"Thank you, your Honor," I said. I had no idea why I was thanking him. Out of habit, I suppose. A police officer pulls you over and gives you a speeding ticket, you thank him. A judge orders you to write a book, you thank him, while cursing at his decision under your breath.

What was this judge—some kind of bibliophile? I thought about my past interactions with Judge Solomon and what I possibly could have done to deserve this. I had seen him at bar functions, in the elevator at the courthouse, and in line at the cafeteria. I had entered a few plea bargains in front of him. Argued a few short motions. I had done nothing to set him off.

At the very least, I decided to vote not to retain the judge in the next election.

A judge is supposed to be fair. Carefully weigh the evidence of each case, the credibility of the witnesses. Apply the applicable law to the facts based on precedent. Craft a reasoned ruling—in the interests of justice. Someone has to make decisions, I understand that. Most judges say they know they have done a good job if neither party is happy with the result. A judge is supposed to be wise. Not issue this crackpot ruling about writing a book.

And who knows what he told his fellow judges about me! Judges hung out together, had morning meetings, attended judicial conferences. Judges went bowling, had barbeques, played badminton together.

Once you were discredited in the eyes of the judges, you were, well, ruined as a trial lawyer. It was so humiliating, I couldn't help but cringe. I thought about what I would say to him if I ever had the opportunity. I needed to get the order set aside. And to find some way to get my revenge.

2

I used to run television ads for my law practice. The Law Firm of Darwyn 'Wyn' VanWye. The ads showed a photo of me with a stupid grin and a phone number. Below me in big letters: 'Call Wyn to Win.' The TV producers made more money off me than I ever did off those ads.

I had looked good in the ads, decked out in my finest pinstriped suit. What Amalia, my ex-wife, who selected it, called my 'killer suit.' Although Amalia knew little about the practice and procedures of law, she was almost always right about the result of any case I discussed with her.

My practice focused on civil litigation and criminal law. Real estate disputes and transactions. Occasional divorces. A business that thrived on the misery of others. I still maintained my real estate broker's license with my company, Wyn Realty. I was that rarity: a real estate attorney who knew something about real estate; a real estate broker who knew something about real estate law.

A Wyn-Wyn, as it were.

My case was adjourned, and the clerk called the next case. In the hallway, I passed people rushing for court from the elevator.

On the first floor, I lingered inside the courthouse by the entrance.

I saw the police officers who ran security with their search tables and x-ray machines, frisking people in suits with a scanner shaped like a wand, heard their voices as they demanded keys and belts and watches. Security was clogged down with lawyers in the line with their big briefcases filled with files and charts and exhibits, the litigants and their witnesses and the lost and confused jurors, with their conspicuous white 'juror' name tags.

When you win a case you gloat, you celebrate, you just do, going over in your head what you did right and why the judge believed you; when you lose a case, you stumble home alone or to a bar in disbelief.

The details of the order were beginning to set in. The judge was out to get me; I was now a sanctioned attorney. Usually when I went to court I felt significant, I stood out. Lost witnesses would ask me directions, and I would direct them to the clerk's office.

At the courthouse, a suit was like a badge or a uniform. The suit was a symbol of success, of being a lawyer, a man of influence. As a matter of pride, I took great care of my suit, laying out my suit coat in the back of my car before every court appearance so it wouldn't get wrinkled. The litigants and jurors usually dressed like they were going to the grocery store. And you could tell what kind of lawyer a person was by the jacket he wore. Private attorneys wore expensive suits; the poorly-paid government lawyers, like public defenders and DAs, wore blazers. Now Judge Solomon had humiliated me with his order; I didn't know how I would ever take another case.

I missed the camaraderie of griping with my fellow attorneys at my old law office. A kind or consoling word from a colleague about the unfairness of Judge Solomon's order. My old office was a real office with land lines, secretaries, paralegals, and a reception area. Even potted plants. I missed the purr of the phones ringing, the clatter of keyboards.

Another thing I missed: books.

Now all I needed to conduct my law practice was my laptop and a smart phone. I met clients at the Starbucks or a sports bar called The Overtime. Occasionally, I even made house calls.

I thought about the order in hopes I could spin it to myself. Like I did for my clients. You take an innocent client to trial, he gets convicted of a crime, and he gets two years probation instead of five years in prison; as a lawyer, you spin it, it's a victory. Another client wants full custody of his child. After a hearing he gets visitation every other weekend; at least he got some parenting time. There was no spin on this one.

I pulled out my phone and googled 'Judge Solomon.' The youngest child of a single mom... worked his way through law school on minimum wage jobs and scholarships... renowned for his empathy... even created a shelter for lost pets... considered knowledgeable, almost 'encyclopedic.'

He had a solid reputation, deftly handling civil and criminal cases as well as certain matters for the Disciplinary Committee. I hoped at least that his wife had left him, and he was miserable.

In his years on the bench, his decisions had never once been overturned. His name was frequently passed around for appointment to the Supreme Court. Worse, he was happily married. For sixteen years.

Judge Solomon had even written an article in a well-respected, influential, and prestigious legal journal about how he had sacrificed a lucrative private law practice to become a distinguished jurist, to leave what he called 'his legacy.'

6

After extensive legal research through Wikipedia, I concluded, much to my astonishment, that Judge Solomon could sentence me to write a book. There was precedent in the state and federal court. Judges had made nutty rulings before, and he had followed them.

There were statutes and rules and there was common law — case law interpreting statutes and rules. Some statutes were interpreted narrowly; others were interpreted liberally.

In other words, a judge could pretty much interpret the law any way he wanted.

3

I checked my phone and noticed that my afternoon appointment had cancelled. The appointment was with a woman who had problems with her landlord. I had tried to help her on the phone, and I assumed by her cancellation she had worked it out. In my normal routine, prospective clients called me all day long, some seeking consultations, some shopping my rates, others wanting free legal advice.

Although my conversations with strangers were protected under the attorney-client privilege, I was amazed that people would leave detailed, confidential, personal messages for me before they retained me. As if based on just contacting me, I was their marriage counselor, psychiatrist, and priest. Lawyer and life-coach. What if it was a wrong number? Or I was opposing counsel? Or whether their version of the facts was so one-sided so as to make defending their case impossible?

Still musing over the judge's order, I drove over to the house in a subdivision called Three Lakes on the south side of town. A small brick wall and a friendly sign for the neighborhood greeted you as you drove in.

It was a good excuse to drop in on Amalia.

The house was a three bedroom. Ready for children. Close to the park. In a family-oriented neighborhood, marked by basketball hoops, Girl Scout troops, and tricycles. I was still paying the mortgage on this house. The house with green trim. The house we bought when we were first married. Now, Amalia's house.

In my head I heard Amalia nagging me about the judge's order. When we talked about my cases, she could figure out who was lying, and I could never pull anything over on her. Usually after spending a few days on a brief or a motion, or a week preparing for a trial, she would ask me about my cases.

She would listen to my facts, which I would carefully explain without revealing anything confidential. I would recite the law, and she would explain what to tell the judge to win the case. Sometimes at breakfast. Sometimes as she packed me a lunch on my way to court.

Even after the divorce, I still loved her. Even despite the alimony. Especially her accent. She was from South America. She said purse when she meant wallet and lock the door instead of close the door. She confused the dishwasher with the dryer. Despite the language obstacles, she had a gift. She would have made a perfect juror.

As I parked in front of the house, I noticed how neatly she had kept the lawn and how good the house looked, giving the impression she was unaffected by the divorce. Her life went on fine, except without me in it. The house had curb appeal — two big bay windows in the front with planters in them. By comparison, much nicer than the home I was squatting in on Hickory Lane. A run-down HUD house. Close to Amalia, but not too close.

First thing I did, I knocked on the door. Nothing worse than walking in on my ex, and I assure you I had the purest intentions. I still had a key left over from the divorce. I knocked again, put my key in the lock, and walked into her home. Shouted out "Hello" like it was a real estate showing.

This was illegal. Arguably.

I only got away with it because (I just remembered) Amalia was at work as a closer for Algonquin Title. A real job. With a salary. Something she adamantly refused to try when we were married.

The house looked the same as when we were married. Each room was painted in a different, bright color, as always. One secondary bedroom pink and the other blue. Boy or girl, she would have been happy either way. When we bought the house, I imagined playing with our children on the swing in the park by the lake. It never happened.

I even wrote down jokes to tell my child: "Who invented the mobile phone?"

I could see my naturally brilliant future little tyke contemplating an answer: "Alexander Graham Cell."

4

If that had worked out, we would probably still be married. And we tried everything—in vitro, fertility drugs, surrogacy, adoption. Say what you will about Amalia, she would have made a wonderful mother.

The builder went broke; no lakes in Three Lakes were ever constructed.

I am not one to become emotionally involved with a home. A home is a real estate investment, nothing more. If it goes bad with a divorce, you just have to let it go.

Amalia and I had chosen the house together and we had struggled with the payments. When we married, we had a simple wedding at the courthouse, with a small reception a few months later. We were that poor. Walking through it now, I noticed that the house had personality. Call it style, call it class, the house was nicely finished. I was unprepared for this. Although it needed carpet, the house still gave me a warm, familiar feeling.

I scoured around the house for a beer. The dining room table and kitchen counter were cluttered with unopened mail and newspaper grocery store coupons. We used to argue about hiring a maid. Because of the economics, maids were common in her

11

country, but I could never afford one here.

Nothing in the kitchen refrigerator. There was no beer anywhere. No luck by the wet bar. I finally looked in the old beer fridge in the garage. I had left some there for entertaining, and found a six-pack.

The garage seemed so empty without the Land Rover. I must say, a car goes safely from A to B, that's all I personally require. Law clients and real estate clients expect a much nicer vehicle, a symbol of success from the advisor they do business with. After all, would you hire an accountant who did your taxes on a manual typewriter and a dusty old calculator?

The Land Rover was a magnificent real estate car. It exuded success. The image of a prosperous lawyer and a real estate broker. It was a beautiful off-white bone color, had a luxurious finish, and was filled with useless high-tech gadgets. It drove smoothly and it could drive pretty much anywhere and in any weather. It had an upgraded stereo, and sometimes I would sit in the garage with the battery on and listen to the music of my youth. Amalia got the car in the divorce. It seemed so unfair because she only drove it to and from work.

With Amalia awarded the Land Rover, I was driving a beaten-up, rusted-out old Ford Festiva. Bright yellow. With a cracked windshield, a broken rear-view mirror and minor hail damage. Brakes scraped as I drove. No doubt a great car back in the '90s, it hobbled from place to place as if gasping for its last breath. Right after the divorce, a law client gave it to me in lieu of my fee. Everyone had a nicer car than me.

I had fond memories of the Land Rover; Amalia did not even learn to drive until I taught her. When we first met, I drove her everywhere, and while I liked the intimacy of being her chauffeur, eventually the distraction affected my business.

When we first bought the car, after teaching her to drive in parking lots and side streets, I placed the speedometer as a joke on 'kilometers.' If my calculations are correct, she drove fifty-five kilometers (or thirty-four miles per hour) in a fifty-five miles per hour speed zone. Cars zoomed past her, people honking, swearing, swerving around her.

"Carajo!" She swore back at the cars in Spanish. "Bush!"

Although I helped her get her American citizenship, as long as I knew her, she refused to participate in politics. But she never got over our forty-third president.

I sat on the garage steps, drinking my second beer (or was it my third?), looking past the empty space for the car, spotting a few of my possessions. My model aircraft carrier, still half-complete, which had been spread out on the dining room table for years. Several law books and old case files still stacked in piles. A broken antique clock. A collection of my old vinyl records—classic rock.

Believe it or not, these records were the highest point of contention in our divorce, which is funny because they had little or no value to anyone except me. This is what we fought over, and she still held them over my head. Not the credit card debt, not the house or the car. Worst of all, I bought most of the records before we were married, and Amalia only went for them because her lawyers knew it would hurt me. In that sense, it was a typical divorce. There was even half a day of testimony about it. I testified in detail about the albums, every single one, how I acquired them, when I acquired them, what they were worth when I bought them, what they were worth now, if anything, for I had to prove in court the marital value of each record, or the increase in value if it was pre-marital, or non-marital such as a gift. In the end, I won on the vinyl, but I had no place to store the records.

In a way, I was hoping she would catch me snooping. Not that she would do anything about it; if I went to jail for criminal trespass, breaking and entering, or burglary, I wouldn't be able to pay her alimony. Besides, I had a defense to these charges: I was still storing some of my personal property in the garage so I was entitled to enter her home.

I still couldn't believe she even let the divorce go so far as to be final. She could have dismissed the divorce at any time, and for this I blame her lawyers. With this in mind, I reached up and dismantled the garage door opener. Not too badly, just so I could come back and repair it. She could park her (my) Land Rover outside. Now this *was* illegal, even criminal. Could be construed as illegal anyway. Arguably. Most likely.

The first time Amalia filed for a divorce, the car broke down. She called me to rescue her, and we got back together. The second time, the waterline to the icemaker on the fridge broke, I came to the rescue. Maybe the third time—this time—really would be the charm.

Not that Amalia couldn't repair the garage door on her own; she wouldn't. I couldn't picture her tiptoeing on a stepladder in her designer dress and stilettos. She did decorate the Three Lakes house.

She was used to people catering to her. After every heavy snow, the retired electrician down the street shoveled the driveway for her. Ever since we first moved into the house. She had smiled at him exactly once. That was all it took.

Amalia took in strays. One spring a homeless man knocked on our door, asked for a job mowing the lawn. She agreed to pay him to do it whenever it was needed. She paid in cash. First, he came every month. Then he came every two weeks. Then every week. Then almost every day. Amalia never flinched and fed him leftovers in the kitchen. The last time he came, he didn't even do the lawn, but he wanted to be paid anyway. Amalia had run out of cash so she wrote him a check—which I put a stop on. That was the last we heard from him. That was the difference between Amalia and me. If she met a homeless man, she assumed he was down on his luck; I assumed he was a dangerous felon who had just escaped from Supermax.

I began to worry about what I had done to the garage door opener.

As a lawyer, I wasn't prepared for the life of a criminal. I was an 'officer of the court.' When I was admitted to the bar, I had sworn an oath to protect my clients and to uphold the laws of the United States and the Constitution.

Besides, there was no point in making her mad. The smallest slight, she would stay mad for days. And if I laughed at her, allured by her passion, she just got madder. It was always very hard to woo her back, and she made me pay dearly.

I immediately tried to repair the garage door opener. Instead, I tangled up the cord. I worked on the cord for a moment longer. The more I tried to fix it, the more messed up it became. I finally gave up. At the very least, she would call me.

If only she would be reasonable. If only we got back together again (I mean, remarry me) or if she agreed, now that she was working for a decent salary—I could get the alimony terminated. It was an outrageous sum I was ordered to pay her: forty-five hundred dollars per month.

First the divorce, the business went down, and because of the alimony, I gave up my office. Now Judge Solomon. What to do about this judge's crazy order? Amalia would know what to do. She would nag me, but she would know.

5

Now I wouldn't have minded the judge's order so much had I done something wrong. That would have been different. It might have been fun to write a book about the dignity and integrity of the legal system. Except now I was ordered to do it. Here I was singled out, without explanation, and that is what set me off. My so-called infraction was officially explained as "conduct that interferes with the administration of justice." I still didn't know what I had done.

Many lawyers stretched the rules of professional ethics, yet few ever got into trouble. We usually had to do something really despicable to be so disgraced. The call from the Disciplinary Committee is the scariest call you can get professionally; it's like the call from the cancer doctor.

The easiest way to be investigated by the Disciplinary Committee is to mismanage your trust account. Collect retainer money from clients and spend it on yourself without doing the work.

It's called stealing.

Or to have sexual contact with your clients. That is simply not allowed. Clients are vulnerable, obviously, especially women, in divorce, revealing their most intimate secrets.

A high profile lawyer was selling meth in exchange for sex with homeless boys. Another lawyer got pulled over for DUI and ran away. He didn't run fast enough. The cops found him hiding in the bushes not a dozen feet from his car. Of course, he denied it, made up some wild story. There was a big fuss about it. On the other hand, I knew an attorney who got suspended simply for swearing in front of a client. The discipline of lawyers was random.

My first thought was to file a motion for reconsideration, and if that failed, an appeal. I looked up the rule. Rule 59 is basically a motion for new trial; it allows you to present newly discovered evidence or argue new theories to show how the judge erred in his original ruling. It also extends the time you have to file an appeal and allows you to build up the record with evidence. In the event, as in my case, the judge had acted like a boob.

6

I've had problems with judges before. I've seen one or two of them fall asleep behind the bench during trial. I had a case where my client asked to go to the bathroom during a hearing. The court denied the request and my client pissed in his pants. The judge wanted to finish the proceeding before lunch. I had a divorce case where in open court the judge called my client fat and lazy. Another case where my client had an affair, and the judge called my client a whore.

Motions for reconsideration under CRCP 59 are usually denied. Judges like to move on, not to revisit the same facts and hear the same case again and again. Usually the court doesn't even rule on the motion, and after sixty-three days, the motion is automatically denied. That leaves the lengthy process of an appeal.

First, for an appeal, or a motion for reconsideration even, you need to order a copy of the record of all the court filings and a transcript of all the hearings. Without a copy of the record, the judge's reasons for his orders are presumed to be correct. I called the clerk to order the transcript. I calculated the date the appeal needed to be filed and wrote it down in my calendar. The court reporters charge by the page, and the quicker you need the transcript, the higher the cost.

I thought about the legal intelligence needed to win it. How could I prove Judge Solomon committed legal error or abused his discretion? In any legal proceeding, you can have identical basic facts, argue the exact same precedent in front of two judges (or the same judge, even) in the same courthouse on the same afternoon and get totally different results.

Judges have made astute rulings in past cases, too. Sifting through facts and correctly applying precedent with amazing precision. I do not say that simply because they ruled in favor of my clients.

I jotted down the numerous mistakes Judge Solomon had made from my memory of the proceeding. Researched precedent. Words like *cruel and unusual punishment. Unconstitutionally vague. Arbitrary and capricious.* These were my best arguments, and I had not even begun to draft a word of it.

Not all of the disciplinary proceedings were as far-fetched as mine. The results of the Disciplinary Committee's more serious investigations were published in a well-respected, influential and prestigious legal journal. As you can imagine, there were lots of complaints against lawyers. Few resulted in disciplinary action.

This was the first section of the journal I read every month as soon as it came out. One judge (not Judge Solomon unfortunately) got disbarred because his wife turned him in for banging a female Deputy Assistant District Attorney. It wasn't just the banging; if a sixty-year-old judge wanted to "refresh his recollection" with a twenty-seven-year-old, good for him. It wasn't about morals. The judge boned her during court recess on the desk in his chambers while she tried active cases before him.

As part of Judge Solomon's ruling, I had to attend an ethics seminar, put on by members of the Disciplinary Committee. As if writing the book wasn't enough of a sanction, I signed up for the official seminar with all the other fallen legal gladiators—savages, really—mostly from small firms or solo practitioners. The larger firms had too much money, no doubt, too much clout to be subjected to such menial punishment.

The ethics seminar took place in a large conference room with no windows on the sixteenth floor of a skyscraper built in the real estate boom of the late '70s. The building was under renovation, and the first thing I noticed, aside from the lack of parking, was that the elevator was slow and clunky. It smelled old.

When I first walked in, I checked in with a secretary next to a table laden with cinnamon buns up for grabs. This was to somehow encourage networking. I took a bun and looked around, but saw no one I knew. No one even said a simple hello. A roomful of strangers sitting under yellow florescent lights, distracted by their laptops and tablets and fancy phones and Bluetooth headphones, sitting in neat rows behind tables, gobbling down their cinnamon rolls, mumbling to themselves like a bunch of homeless people in suits.

The seminar began with a lot of introductions by members of the Disciplinary Committee. Humiliated by the fact of being falsely accused, I was forced to sit through maybe ten minutes of useful information in a boring presentation that started early in the morning and lasted all afternoon. No matter what I had done, wasn't that punishment enough?

"There are no dumb questions," a woman from the Disciplinary Committee who never even practiced law, announced.

Some guy with a beard raised his hand. "Does the rule against sexual contact with a client apply to oral sex?"

I was tempted to raise my hand. Not to be so bold as to contradict the Committee, but that was a dumb question. Of course, oral sex was sex. And what did it matter? As if without this rule—and without cash or certified check—this wrinkled old fat fool was going to get some babe to go down on him. Some people are just creepy.

Upon interviewing this transgressor during one of the breaks, I discovered he had not actually violated any of the Committee's rules of professional ethics regarding sexual contact with a client. He'd had sex with the woman, who was his ex-girlfriend, *before* he represented her. There was no rule against continuing a sexual relationship that existed before the woman became a client, just against taking advantage of the attorney-client relationship to start a sexual relationship with a client. His problem was his billing activities. These sexual escapades occurred in his office and his monthly invoices reflected he had billed her for his time for what could most politely be described between the two of them as non-legal personal services.

Now charging attorney's fees for a deposition that never took place; falsifying the date of service on a pleading so it wouldn't be late. Refusing to pay the court reporter the costs of a transcript. Failing to return a client's file. Now those are infractions.

These were some of the reprehensible allegations floating around against the lawyers there. Posed as a hypothetical, after chatting with many of the other attorneys at the beginning, during, and end of the seminar, no one thought Judge Solomon's order against me was justified.

After I conducted my own private investigation—interviewing

the remaining noble advocates about their alleged crimes—I was comforted by the remarkable fact that not a single lawyer sentenced to suffer through this ethics seminar had committed the infraction of which he was so wrongfully accused.

7

In my reflections about the order, I began to consider what I knew about ethics and the *Rules of Professional Conduct* which I learned in law school. At the time I applied to law school, I was unsettled, skeptical about becoming a lawyer. I had my reasons.

After an enormously successful year as a real estate broker, I was inexplicably sad. I paced around the Three Lakes house oddly dissatisfied with myself. As much as I enjoyed the real estate business, it had its ups and downs. Financial problems usually led to fights with Amalia, and I sought a solution. Or maybe I was bored. Was this beautiful life with my beautiful wife all that there was? Of all the fellow real estate brokers I spoke to, busy as they were making cold calls, holding open houses, playing golf with clients or each other, and closing deals, no one felt sorry for me.

I was getting older, yes, that's what it was. I needed the security for Amalia and security to start my family, and I convinced myself I was ready for a change. But the profession of law seemed so respectable, so adult. I wasn't sure I was ready for that. The sadder and more dissatisfied I became, the more I wanted to become an attorney.

I soon realized that law school wouldn't really solve anything, but I became obsessed with applying. I researched law schools, prepped for the LSAT, ordered my college transcripts, requested letters of recommendation, checked admission standards, grants, student loans, and scholarship applications. Why not go? Amalia finally advised me to try, fed up with my moping and personal deliberations. I would get old regardless, she explained, and so I jumped.

Before law school, I'd had my own encounters in the court system. I often got traffic tickets en route to real estate appointments, and I had once or twice hired a lawyer named Traffic Jack to handle the violations. He was the legal guru of traffic cases. Most of my charges were minor speeding tickets.

Once I got a ticket for showing a Spanish couple houses for sale in a nice suburban neighborhood. No, seriously, I was driving this couple and their kids around in an area called Highlands Ranch when a cop followed me from the first house I showed to the next, and finally pulled me over. He couldn't find anything to charge me with so he charged me for the way I pulled over and stopped when he pulled me over. Traffic Jack took care of it.

All he handled were traffic cases, and he was good at them, scheduling them in Algonquin County all at the same time in order to make his caseload manageable. An older man, he usually wore a very expensive black suit adorned with a silk red handkerchief in the front pocket to make himself appear sophisticated. At the conclusion of every one of my plea-bargained citations, he sent me a detailed and outrageous bill, explaining the potential consequences of the charges against me, the risk of serious jail time for minor traffic violations, the high level of skill required for his negotiations, and praising himself for 'saving' my driver's license.

I later learned as a lawyer—as I suspected—that Traffic Jack was full of himself. Negotiations on minor traffic violations are easy, and the deals are pretty standard. Lesson learned.

Several of my real estate clients who were lawyers warned me not to apply to law school. It would ruin me, they said. They themselves wanted to quit their jobs as high-powered attorneys and partners at big firms and sell real estate as I did. Or even work in the farmer's market. One wanted to become a mailman. Another wanted to invest with me in buying a Dairy Queen. A third one said I wasn't smart enough and that I would never make it. It seemed like these attorneys were simply trying to keep me out, keep the erudite and esoteric attorney world secret.

That made me want to apply even more.

At quiet dinner parties with some of these lawyers and their wives, I played Trivial Pursuit and Scrabble, and I must say, in my opinion, despite their arrogance, they were clearly not much smarter than I was. I could see myself walking alongside a disgraced politician like they did, answering questions with the press, or simply saying "No Comment." Or pontificating about legal issues as a guest expert on television, sitting next to the rather fetching weather girl on the news team on Channel 9.

As I mulled through the possibilities, there were advantages to a law career I had never considered before, and once I considered them, it became clear to me that probably I should have considered them all along. All of a sudden, it occurred to me that I might still have a future other than just as a real estate broker.

What really got me interested in law was Donald Douglas Trickey. And yes, that is his real name; he still practices here. He was a very fine lawyer and I mean that in the worst possible way. A master of running up billable hours. Dignified, precise. Unbelievably nice.

I had acted as a broker for a couple who moved here from Richmond, Virginia. After several house-hunting trips, showing dozens of houses and providing lunches and dinners and personal tours of the city, I found them one they liked in an area of gently rolling hills down on the southeast side of town. The couple submitted an offer with a quick close, and the offer was accepted without even a counterproposal. The home passed inspection and appraisal, the buyers had twenty per cent as a down payment, the loan was approved, and they were ready to close. Their furniture was scheduled to arrive on two big Mayflower moving trucks after the closing. The transaction was going fine, until the buyers hired Trickey.

Trickey was the buyer's attorney, retained only for the closing. Although Trickey had received the closing documents well in advance, he had not bothered to review them. After several hours reading and discussing them at the closing table at Algonquin Title, running up his bill, he insisted on changing the language on a standard loan document. A federal form.

"No one can do that," I explained. "It's a government form. You either sign the docs or you don't close."

"Are you an attorney?" Attorney Donald Douglas Trickey asked.

"No, just the broker."

"Then be quiet, please."

Lawyers and brokers are natural enemies. A broker wants to do the deal; a lawyer wants to kill the deal. A lawyer nitpicks every detail. The more problems he creates, the more money he makes. A real estate broker makes the same amount at closing no matter how long the deal takes.

A lawyer asks: What if? A broker asks: Why not?

Upon the advice of Trickey, the buyers refused to sign the loan documents. The seller refused to grant an extension of time to allow Trickey time to get them modified. The deal died. There was a big brouhaha over the earnest money.

What struck me as I walked away from the failed closing is how Trickey did not listen to the needs of his client. Not one bit. He did not give a whit. The buyers were anxious to move in, their furniture overloaded on the two Mayflower trucks.

There was cable to be activated, keys to the community pool. Jobs to report to, kids to be enrolled in school. I mean, really, he gave bad advice. After all that fuss, the seller simply sold the house to someone else for a higher price.

That is the exact moment I decided to become an attorney. When I felt that spark. Trickey and that failed real estate closing. The buyers lost their earnest money; they were forced to rent a home for a while. After all that work, showing homes to out-of-town buyers, I went to the closing expecting a big check, and walked away with nothing. For his bad advice, Trickey, the deal-killer, earned a thousand dollars.

I could have sabotaged the deal for a lot less than that.

I still see Trickey's name sometimes on internet ads for his law practice. I always check out the ad, hoping it is a "pay per click" for having space on the internet, and each click will cost Trickey money.

Sometimes I click on it twice.

8

In my essay for admission to law school, I wrote about how the middle class needed a lawyer, and I could be that lawyer at a reasonable fee. I could protect the tenant from being wrongly evicted. The real estate broker denied a commission. The buyer unjustly forfeiting his earnest money deposit. At the time I meant it, I believed it, I was sincere. I was ready to do battle. Amalia read my essay, gathered up my application, and mailed it off to the admissions department. Of the two law schools in our state, only one offered night classes. Much to my surprise, my acceptance to law school came a few months later.

The first event in law school, you are welcomed at orientation by the faculty and congratulated for choosing the field of law over all the other professions, and of course, their prestigious school. The study of law is a noble calling. It is a daunting responsibility. The opportunity to make a real difference in people's lives. To persuade a judge or a jury to right some wrong. The case can become precedent for similar cases that follow. The world is a better, safer place because of lawyers. Automobiles are safer, trains are safer, medications are better tested, because of lawyers. Lawyers are more influential than any other professional. An engineer? Mere math. A scientist. Physics, biology, chemistry. A physician can help people, too, but all he does is diagnose symptoms and concoct remedies. Nothing that hard about it. His job is trial or error. He is like a chef, looking up symptoms like recipes. A chef wears a toque, a doctor wears a smock. A lawyer is technically a doctor anyway; the law degree is a juris doctorate degree, and in law school the professors refer to you as 'doctor.'

Not even Albert Einstein was smart enough to become an attorney.

If you ever get the opportunity to go to law school, you should take it. It will change the way you think, the way you view the world. It will solve your money problems because while there are not always jobs, there is always work, always people who need legal advice, always couples who hate each other.

I have heard of starving artists—I've even known artists who live their whole lives and never sell a single painting. I've never met a starving attorney. And I haven't had a traffic violation that stuck for years.

Finally, when you get your law degree, your parents will be proud. That's worth a lifetime burden of student loans right there. The way I did it, at night school, you need to finish law school in five years.

The law students in my classes: women with brains and big thick glasses; the nerdy boy above his peers, clothes his mother bought at Sears. Some students came to law school to learn to prosecute criminals so they could put people in jail—the path to becoming a partner in a litigation firm or ultimately, a judge. Others were failed actors, wanting to show off their talents in front of a jury. There were a few paralegals, tired of doing all the work and being paid as secretaries. One or two were bored.

There were no working class heroes. No constitutional

scholars. The students in my class just wanted dollars.

The course work was easier than I had anticipated. The first thing I learned was how to "think like a lawyer." The basic concepts of legal analysis had an acronym: I-R-A-C. Issue, Rule, Analysis, Conclusion.

I learned how to book brief cases. Spot the legal issue and apply the facts, ignoring the details that have no legal consequence. Underline the factors with a four-colored pen. Red for the issue, green for the rule of law, etc. In other words, I finally got to draw in the books we read. Coloring for grownups. Seriously. A kindergartner could do it.

I memorized amusing anecdotes I could show off at parties. Stories I could tell to my future children just to see them roll their little eyes.

For example, one of the most influential and famous cases in legal history was not about civil rights or the Constitution. It was not a big scandal. The ruling did not result in a big reversal or result in a huge monetary judgment. It was probably not even newsworthy.

It was the Palsgraf case, the case of a bystander who was injured when a man running for a train accidentally dropped a package containing fireworks that exploded. The case set the precedent limiting liability for all negligence claims to whether the incident that causes injury was foreseeable.

Did you know, in English law, if a ship was shipwrecked on a deserted island and the crew was stranded without food, the crew killed and ate the tasty young cabin boy? The defense of choice of evils allowed the crew—after much outrage, publicity, weight loss, and an extensive trial—to go free because the consumption of the cabin boy was necessary for the crew's survival and therefore justified.

When trains were first invented, there was no body of law to consider their risks so the courts applied the negligence and nuisance laws of harboring wild animals.

And in jolly old England, when there was a real estate transaction, the seller of the property tossed the sod from the grounds of the estate at the buyer's feet as a symbol of the deal. The deal needed a witness—a peasant boy was beaten, almost to death—so he would remember. This proved so highly inefficient, the statute of frauds evolved, requiring that the terms of a real estate transaction to be in writing.

Law school changed me, it pulled out the weak in me, broke me, and rebuilt me. I learned how to defend myself, which would enable me to defend my clients. In my last year, I took classes in trial practice and moot court. Studied the cross examination and closing techniques of famous lawyers.

I wrote wonderful thoughtful provocative briefs quoting the great minds of Jefferson and Madison. Oliver Wendell Holmes, Bono, Richard Milhous Nixon. Studied concepts like Due Process, Equal Protection and Justice. I learned later, these lofty concepts had nothing to do with the actual practice of law.

Back then, I was surprised by some of these concepts. I studied, among other books, *Black's Law Dictionary.* I was initially confused as to whether it contained separate but unequal laws for African Americans and other minorities. You would naturally think there were separate laws—judging by the book's title and the disproportionate high number of African Americans and Mexicans in prison. Surprisingly, the law is supposed to be applied the same, regardless of race, religion, and national origin. It's in that often overlooked crumpled-up old document, the U.S.

Constitution. The right to be judged not by the color of your skin but by the quality of your attorney.

I had a ridiculously high bar score, but unlike in the movies, nobody cared.

As a final requirement for acceptance into the bar, I had to pass a character check. I was required to candidly disclose my character flaws and explain — no, justify — any of my past conduct that could show me unfit to bear the torch of justice. Honestly, I could have written a book about that.

I needed to explain past lawsuits and judgments. Bankruptcies, which are perfectly legal and should not even be considered. Criminal activity whether or not convicted. Every single time in college I accidentally smoked pot. Whether I inhaled or not. (No one actually disclosed this.) Even conviction of a violent felony can be overlooked if enough time has passed and you know how to grovel.

There was one bar candidate from my class who did quite well in law school, passed the bar the first time out, and landed a good job as an associate at a big downtown law firm, subject to admission to the bar. To celebrate, he and his closest friends and neighbors decided to go to a sports event.

He collected money from his neighbors for Broncos tickets, and then pocketed the cash, never buying the tickets. That was a deplorable act of moral turpitude, depravity and high treason, and the candidate disclosed it on his bar application. He was denied admission. Just for being a bonehead.

Law school fulfilled some emptiness in me. To me, lawyers were among the chosen. The gatekeepers of truth. The ones with a purpose. I could now confidently babble on about subjects I knew absolutely nothing about. I worked all day, went to law school at night, read thick law books in the library, and slogged home to be with Amalia.

9

I agonized about what I had done to Amalia's garage door opener for the next few days. I drove by the Three Lakes house, checking to see if the Land Rover was parked in the driveway. Nothing each time. Not in the morning, not after lunch at The Overtime, not even at night. Finally, I sought Amalia out at her work.

Algonquin Title was located in a posh part of town, populated with bungalows from the twenties, old apartments renovated into condos, new high-end townhomes, and luxury boutiques surrounding an overpriced and congested shopping mall. It was a bland white building made of concrete and steel, an eyesore with small rectangular windows, a remnant of the architecture of the Cold War.

As I parked, I noticed the Land Rover, confirming at least, that Amalia was at her office. I was a little relieved. It was a strange time to be alive, with the twenty-four hour news channels of bad news. You could drop your child at your neighborhood high school, only for the child to be injured in a school shooting. You could go to a movie premiere, only to be terrorized by a crazed gunman who sprays bullets across the theater.

Walking toward the building through the parking lot, I

wondered how Amalia and I ended up this way. If she ever thought of me the way I thought of her.

We were young when we met, we were both in our late-twenties. I met her at an open house; she walked in with one of her aunts. She signed the guest register book I used as a broker to get leads. I followed up. She wasn't ready to buy, and, after talking to her a few times, eventually I asked her out to lunch.

As I said, when we first met, she didn't drive; our early life together was filled with the intimacy of small errands. I drove her to her job as a seamstress performing alterations on the west side of town in the mornings and picked her up after work so she wouldn't have to take the bus. I liked to think of that time period as a much happier, simpler time. We must have been compatible because even as her mere chauffeur I was content to hang with her at the Laundromat, the dentist's office, shop arm-in-arm with her at the grocery store, or wait in a chair at a retail store while she went clothes shopping.

It was amazing that we ever got together in the first place. Amalia and I didn't really have that much in common. She liked spicy food and Spanish folk music and American disco, and dancing from salsa to samba. And she loved Three Dog Night, of all things. ("Jeremiah was a Bullfrog," she would sing, and "One is the Loneliest Number.") Liked *Kojak* reruns and shows from the seventies she saw when she was growing up. She thought the Clash was a fashion statement and Social Distortion a bunch of noise. She would rescue an old avocado green refrigerator from the dumpster like she had found some great treasure. If she met you walking your dog, she might pet your dog, she might sing to your dog, she might bark at it. Sometimes at the movies she laughed so loud and awkwardly that people laughed at her laughter. If the movie featured a song she knew, she would forget where she was and sing along. She was puzzling and unpredictable. Simple yet complex. Fascinating yet frustrating. In other words, she was the love of my life.

In our eighteen years of marriage, I had never learned Spanish, and that was another one of my regrets. I had learned a lot about her country, but I had never traveled there. I was never free for travel. The curse of the self-employed. Always helping clients, seeking new clients, or soliciting business from past clients. But I learned that green cards weren't necessarily green and that the best Spanish soap operas were in Portuguese.

Amalia and I eventually wanted to retire in Buenos Aires, and we talked about me taking Spanish lessons. Because of the divorce, I would never retire on purpose. Instead, I will retire by chance. I will die from a heart attack while showing tract houses in Highlands Ranch.

Amalia liked to argue, and in that regard we made a cute couple. She didn't like to be alone, so she kept the TV on for company, flipping through several shows at the same time. Once she saw a documentary (mock-u-mentary) about mermaids discovered in the South Pacific, and she swore it was true.

Another time she saw a television news broadcast about a rabid bat found near a lake. The Department of Health issued a warning, looking for anyone who had come into contact with the infected animal. It was a serious health risk, and it was repeated several times on the local channels as breaking news.

She believed in mermaids but she couldn't believe this. She flipped from channel to channel trying to keep up with the progress in the story.

"A rabbit-bat!" She made a hopping gesture with two fingers. "A tiny bat with big teeth and floppy ears. You gringos, what you will think of."

As much as I tried to explain that it was simply a contagiously diseased bat, she didn't believe me. We argued for hours about the existence of this scientifically genetically-altered animal.

Astonishing. Ever since the first moonwalk, she was suspicious about the veracity of American scientific advances. You would think disagreeing with her was a capital crime.

"We'll go to the zoo," I said, finally giving in, "and see the rabbit-bats. While we are there, we can see the mermaids and the rabbit-squirrels, too."

Another thing she loved, shopping. She shopped for me and for all of her cousins she hadn't seen in years back in Argentina. She collected old discarded cell phones for some reason and sent them back there. She frequented several malls which all looked alike to me, but she watched the sales and was often drawn in.

She had a thing for shoes. I remember one year, she got all excited, a woman was running for president. All she could talk about was supporting this female candidate. Day and night, she went on about this woman. The day the woman came to Algonquin County to give a speech, Amalia decked herself out and drove down to hear her speak. On the way, Amalia stopped at the grand opening of a new mall. After all that fuss, she got so carried away in the woman's shoe department, she missed the candidate's rally.

One time, I think it was around Christmas, she wanted to buy some boots. As we walked through the stores in the mall, the boots were ridiculously expensive. At one store, I saw a sign that offered the boots at half price — buy one get one free. I offered to buy one boot at half price, get the second one for free.

They were called Uggs. Even their name was ugly.

"No one buys just one boot," surmised the clerk at the cashier's counter.

"Well, I do," I argued. "That's what the sign says."

I took the sign from the display and plopped it in front of the cashier.

"See," I explained, proudly. "Exhibit A. In big bold letters. Buy One, Get One Free. It doesn't say you have to buy two."

The clerk and I argued for about an hour. I explained the intricacies of the Consumer Protection Act and the consequences of false advertising. Finally the clerk got so frustrated, she threw the boots at me, and the boots were free. I think Amalia still has them.

As much as she liked dining out at expensive restaurants, or making recipes with exotic food, she was sometimes happy with a box of Fig Newtons. Whenever these memories flooded me, I thought we should start dating again.

10

I had used this title company for years. Although the building looked like a bomb shelter, the inside was upscale and inviting. There was a reception area littered with real estate brokers, buyers and sellers waiting for their closings, and an attractive young secretary offering free Coke or coffee. There were several small conference rooms for closings with complimentary pens, and in the back cubicles filled with desks and phones and office equipment where the closers prepared the real estate documents.

I was largely responsible for Amalia's job there. Her country didn't encourage the education of its children as much as ours, so she had no formal higher education. Before she was a seamstress here, she had lived in a college town for a year or two with an aunt (Tia Dorito, that was her aunt's name) in Manhattan, Kansas. The Little Apple. She moved here with another one of her aunts who died soon after we got married.

Amalia was amazed at our busy congested streets, the tract houses built on small lots with no trees, the cars with ski racks on their roofs that were easily confused with police cruisers. Toward the end of our marriage, she decided to try a job answering phones at the title company and was soon promoted to processor, a job she learned quickly. As a processor, she developed her computer skills, she was fluent in Spanish, and she quickly rose to the position of closer. Besides, people naturally liked her.

As I walked past the receptionist desk at the title company, I smiled when I saw her in her cubicle. She was polite and civilized, almost too civilized, that is, except when she got with her lawyers; then she became intolerable. Our divorce had been stressful and disconcerting. She still dressed flashy, like when we were married, but professional now, and she had gained a little weight, which I knew bothered her. She had a history of dieting obsessively, and then, all of a sudden, back on the Dunkin!

Probably the Fig Newtons.

I still saw her as the bright, dark-skinned, cute curly-haired girl I had married. No matter how complicated and difficult she had become, given the chance, I would still sleep with her. And "irregardless," as Judge Tezak used to say, I would pick her as my closer every time.

I was disappointed I hadn't heard from her. Probably the annoying neighbor had fixed the garage door opener. Just as well. I was tired of worrying about it—and circling by her house and her office in my noisy Festiva three times a day.

"You!" she said, when she saw me. It was more like a growl. "What can I do for you? I have a 3 o'clock closing."

She used her professional voice. She had a professional voice and a casual voice, something she mastered in training. Wham! The way she said it, it was like we were married again, if only for a moment.

I was suddenly too embarrassed to ask her out. I still owed her alimony. I had waited on a real estate closing which was delayed. Real estate deals can be emotionally charged, and often a small detail can escalate a transaction. The buyers and sellers had argued over an electric can opener. They must have both liked tuna fish. Was the electric can opener attached — a fixture and therefore included in the sale — or was it personal property, and the sellers could take it with them? This evolved into a significant dispute, a real estate and legal issue, and the deal almost died because of it.

By the time the deal closed, the money I reserved for her alimony went to pay bills, and the money was gone. It wasn't like she really even needed the money anyway, having gotten virtually all of the assets — and none of the debt — in the divorce.

When I told her about the judge's order about writing a book, I immediately regretted it. I would never hear the end of it. I expected her to listen to my legal arguments. At least say the judge's order was wrong.

"Don't be an idiot," she said. "If a judge orders you to write a book, write the book. Case closed. This is why you are always in the troubles, Vanderbilt boy. What else didn't they teach you?

"It's your mouth that always gets you in trouble," she went on, gleefully. "The fish dies by the mouth."

This was one of her intriguing, charming, but nonsensical phrases. She looked at her watch and nodded, took her files and her mug swirling with fresh coffee and went into her closing.

11

Generally, a simple real estate closing takes about an hour. The parties go over the settlement statements and closing documents; the seller, without reading them, signs a general warranty deed, a bill of sale and a few other forms; and, without reading them, the buyer signs the loan documents. The title company notarizes the warranty deed, copies the photo IDs, the money is exchanged, and the deal closes.

That is, except when lawyers are invited. Drat! Then the closing documents are read, even studied; there are explanations, discussions, and arguments, about every single form. I noticed several lawyers entered into Amalia's closing so I ended the conversation with Amalia where she had left it and drove out to The Overtime.

I thought about my conversation with Amalia. She had several nicknames for me. Vanderbilt Boy. Gordo. Gringo. To name a few. Amalia held my pedigree against me. She only found out about it because my old undergrad college doggedly pursued me for alumni contributions. I went to law school at a more affordable, less-known state college.

Imagine, one of the richest and most expensive schools in the country tracking me down for money!

The name didn't do me much good, anyway. Outside of the South, Vanderbilt was mostly famous for basketball—and jeans, which had nothing to do with the college. There I was squatting in a repossessed HUD home.

As a broker, I had seen so many houses I could look past the cracked windows and the cat smell in the carpet. I had seen worse, much worse. The government owned hundreds of vacant houses, and with the alimony I couldn't afford an apartment.

This was illegal. You could argue. Most likely.

What did I look for in a home, even if it was as a squatter? I liked two-stories better than ranches. A nice open floor plan. Newer carpet. With a private yard. Pet free, Smoke Free. Priced way too high, so it wouldn't sell. Quiet at night. With vaulted ceilings. Lots of natural light.

The home where I squatted was more or less perfect. Except the home did not have air conditioning. A nice house with a newer kitchen and a small yard. As I said, it was close to Amalia, but not too close.

I had other problems, too. My business was down, because of depression and the divorce. I hadn't reported my income in several years, collecting my legal fees in cash and not paying taxes. Illegal. Arguably.

Although I remembered what Amalia had said, I was still considering the appeal. Judge Solomon's ruling against me was all about principle. Questions of right and wrong. Principle had no place in the practice of law.

Then there was the question: what if I won the appeal?

I studied precedent about a poor inmate, appealing his

twenty-year sentence for felony murder. He submitted his best arguments, mostly legal technicalities. When he finally won the appeal, he was ecstatic. In a written ruling by the Court of Appeals, the judge was sharply criticized for his errors in reasoning, exposed as an idiot, and the case remanded for a new trial.

With the same judge.

At the new trial the inmate lost again, but the judge graciously admitted he made mistakes in the first trial, gave him credit for the time he served; he even apologized profusely, which is unheard of. The inmate asked the judge to overturn the verdict, which—with a faint smile—the judge denied. He pleaded for mercy because, quite simply, he was innocent, he did not commit the crime. The judge found that it didn't matter if he didn't do the crime, he was legally guilty, and that was now a legal fact; the jury found him guilty—not only once but twice.

The inmate begged for leniency because he had children. The judge ruled that pleading for leniency because you have children is even more aggravating; the more you have, the more you have to lose. In fact, upon further review of aggravating factors revealed in the new trial, the judge upped the sentence from twenty to thirty-six years.

As I continued my legal analysis, it became perfectly clear: the worst thing that could happen to me—I win the appeal. Who knows what would happen? What other crazy order could I get? What if the new order upped the book to eighty thousand words?

In the meanwhile, the order remained in place. Even if I filed the appeal, I still had to write the book while the appeal was pending.

Besides, I never heard back from the clerk about the transcript.

When I called the clerk again, I counted the days remaining. Something was wrong with the math; I counted the days on my calendar for a third time.

I let the date pass for filing the appeal. A hard deadline.

Forget the appeal. I was worried about my next meal.

Maybe I would vote for him.

At least now I had something I could live with. And no one was paying me for all these billable hours.

12

About writing the book, you'd think it would be an easy task for a lawyer. Most lawyers had stories to tell, explaining in colorful and grandiose detail how they saved the day, won the big case, freed an innocent man wrongly convicted of murder, or defeated a big insurance company.

Good stories all, obviously, and excellently written. After all, lawyers wrote them.

All the lawyers I knew had a novel or a screenplay they were working on. Look in any lawyer's office. Behind the stacks of statutes, *Black's Law Dictionary*, legal journals and articles about the US Constitution, on the bookshelf somewhere would be an old edition of the *Writer's Market*.

Every lawyer dreams of winning 'the one big case.' The windfall. Writing a best-selling book and making a movie deal, followed maybe by a television interview with celebrated journalists like Jon Stewart or Stephen Colbert.

I had yet to see that case.

In my career as a lawyer, I had taken on one of the smaller cities whose city council was directly involved in a high-end development. The architect for the project was also the city planner, and rather than be exposed, I made them scale down the development and move a road.

In another case, I had sued a physician and a big pharmacy for selling narcotics to teenagers on the internet without valid prescriptions. That case went on for several years. I nicknamed that internet doctor 'Dr. Pill.'

Another time, I had represented a client who owned twenty-nine failing retail malls in real estate disputes. I definitely had some big clients and big cases. But most of my cases were small and boring.

When I first got my license, I was fearless, ready to take on anyone. Car dealerships, mortgage companies, banks. Utility companies, cell phone companies. Insurance companies, home warranty companies. I had a list. A new lawyer unleashed upon the world.

It was strange that doctors, engineers, real estate brokers, and appraisers have to complete an internship under an experienced professional, but a lawyer can practice — or commit malpractice — straight out of law school.

As a new lawyer, I saw injustice everywhere. If my library books were overdue, no matter how small the penalties, I was entitled to Due Process. I demanded a hearing on the reasonableness of the fines. I argued at the customer service counter at Walmart over the deceptively advertised price of paper towels.

When I took a case, I always assumed I was going to take the case to trial. I always assumed I would win the case. The law and the rules of civil procedure were my weapons, the evidence my arsenal.

I was a soldier, a warrior, a chieftain; it's a game of chess, to some extent, a game of Risk and the risk is that whatever strategy I chose could backfire and hurt my client's case. I was a man of war.

A female attorney is a woman of war. Somehow that doesn't sound quite as strong.

In one case, during a permanent orders hearing for a divorce, my client's soon-to-be ex suffered a minor stroke on the stand. A petit mal. I had called him first as my witness so it would throw him off his testimony.

The purpose of cross examination is to make the witness lie or look stupid. Here I succeeded. Soon after I began to question him, he sat there on the stand, frozen in a daze. The ambulance was called, he was carried out in a stretcher, and the case was continued.

This was the highlight of my year.

Months later, when the hearing resumed, and I continued to question the husband, the opposing counsel objected.

"Your Honor," he said. "Mr. TV Guy is trying to give my client a seizure — again."

Mr. TV Guy. I thought that description was funny. Those ads were years ago, but they had made me a kind of a celebrity. It was supposed to be insulting. I didn't care what opposing counsel called me or why I won. As long as I won.

I was my own weapon of mass destruction. I sent emails to opposing counsel in the middle of the night so they would think I was working on the case. Jammed their fax machines with hundreds of pages of documents. Teased and taunted them into settling. I've never heard a client say he liked his lawyer because he tried hard. Only that he liked his lawyer because he won.

In one case, there was an opposing counsel in a civil case, I forgot his name but his initials were B.S. I know lawyers are supposed to zealously represent their client. This lawyer was excessive. He was rude and impatient and always misstating and exaggerating the facts of the case. He refused to agree to an extension of time for several motions, except for the one time he agreed to a continuance in exchange for me granting him an extension. He routinely would file court filings without sending me a copy even though he certified in the pleadings he had mailed the filings; I periodically had to go down to the courthouse to review the court file to see if he had filed anything. His name was so common, his email address was BS@BSlaw.com.

The first email I sent him (and email was new to me), I wrote, Dear Mr. B.S. —; I did this throughout the case, I mean, his initials were B.S. — until he threatened to call the bar association on me.

The only one of my cases that had some flare was my Superman case. Not the real Superman, of course, though that might be more lucrative. Damages from cars tossed, buildings lost. A suit against Batman, the billionaire, would be even better.

He called himself Dodgeman, which was (confusingly) similar to Superman. I'm sure you've seen his television commercials. The pudgy, dark-haired owner of a Dodge dealership, decked out in his red and blue tights, flying with his arms straight out above the roofs of the cars in his dealership on the screen — offering 'super' deals.

My client sued him for setting back the odometer on his purchase of a used blue minivan. Unconscionable. Unforgivable. Egregious. Call the lieutenant governor, the deputy mayor!

It was a tough case. Dodgeman put up a hell of a fight. He refused to settle the case. In those cases, you don't threaten them.

You don't make fun of them. Working day and night, doing research, investigating facts, interviewing witnesses, and finding precedent, you beat them.

In a civil case, you have to prove *damages*. Something to always consider. What are your damages and what is the likelihood of the Defendant having the wherewithal to pay the damages? A contract claim is limited in damages to the 'benefit of the bargain.' A personal injury claim is virtually unlimited in damages, though reduced by the percentage of your own negligence. If the jury finds you were partially at fault, your verdict is reduced by that percentage. If the jury finds you were half at fault or more, the damages are reduced to zero. This is called comparative negligence.

The damages here were the difference in the value of the van with the miles promised as compared to the value of the van with the miles actually on the car. My client was entitled to what he bargained for.

Nothing less, nothing more.

After extensive and sincere deliberations by an erratic and unpredictable jury that was mentally tortured for five days by being forced to listen to the opening and closing arguments, the photos and expert reports regarding a used Dodge Caravan, tedious, repetitive testimony and cross examinations, nitpicking objections, and going over the jury instructions, the jury awarded the buyers a damages award of one dollar.

In other words, after weeks of discovery, motions, and depositions, and a five-day jury trial, I won, hands down. A big victory. Already one off the list.

The dealership's license was suspended for a whole afternoon.

There was some publicity about it. For a while, I was called

51

'The Kryptonite Counselor.' 'The Superman Slayer.' It was like I had won the lottery. Justice rocked!

13

Although I had defeated Superman, I couldn't beat Judge Solomon.

I was now stuck with this project.

It was late September, the leaves were turning in the foothills. It was the high season for the Broncos, already snow in the mountains, and the deadlines for additional legal maneuvering had already passed.

The book had to be about the dignity and integrity of the legal system. Dignity meant civility and decorum. Integrity had to mean the fairness of how the system functioned.

I would write a memoir. To satisfy the order.

For law students, lawyers, and other criminals. Not about dignity and integrity, exactly. A guidebook, if you will. Filled with insights into truth and justice and told with intelligent humor. Write about what you know. The trade secrets of practicing law.

Not about how to win the big case, but how to lose the little ones.

14

Now that I made a decision about following the Judge's order, I could concentrate on my law practice. Although I still missed the attractions of my old law office, I liked meeting clients at The Overtime. High ceilings with spinning colored fans. Walls decorated with glaring big screen televisions. Rock songs from '70s and early '80s.

I preferred to hold meetings with prospective clients in the dining section. It seemed more professional than the raucous sports bar.

The manager, Kendall, had both an undergraduate and masters degree in restaurant, hotel, and casino hospitality from some university in Las Vegas. Can you imagine a university in Vegas... I bet you there is one. With those qualifications, after months of handing out resumes and going to job interviews, he was finally able to land a job as manager of a local bar. He was one of these naturally laid-back dusty-blonde guys with casual clothes and well-groomed, yet slightly unkempt hair. He looked and dressed like a singer-songwriter from the '70s. He had good luck with women, but bad luck because it was with the wrong women. The bar was occasionally shadowed with drama — intense whispers at dark corner tables between Kendall and his latest dalliance.

Kendall had one of those nightmare divorces, a goldmine for lawyers. As a result, he had developed an odd sense of humor which no one took seriously. It was like he was punishing himself for the divorce. I knew the feeling from my own divorce, and with my talks with Kendall I could talk about Amalia.

I know a divorce in our state is a "no-fault" divorce, but for my divorce I blamed Amalia. Our life together was good and it was never clear to me why she ended the marriage. I had worked hard to pay the bills, and she had enjoyed the lifestyle I provided. So much so that often when I was tied up showing houses or preparing for trial, she would go out with her friends.

She was involved in the South American community, and that meant attending teas and playing canasta with old ladies and an occasional festival or party. Once, after not going with her to these events for several years, I surprised her, dressed up, and accompanied her to a party. When Amalia introduced me as her husband, more than one of her friends congratulated her on the wedding. Although we had been married for years, some of the ladies at the party thought — after seeing her come alone for so long at similar events — that she was single. Not once did I complain about her going to these outings.

Kendall's X had named their small son Henry Louis. He sometimes played in the back room at the bar during Kendall's parenting time. Named after her father. Not just Henry. Henry Louis. No first name without the middle name. Not a nickname. Not ever. Kendall had called him Hank once. She was so furious, so outraged, she filed a motion.

He liked to joke about murdering his ex-wife. On planning an elk hunting trip with some of the regulars, he mentioned looking for a nice remote spot in the mountains to bury the body. Even joked about going to Sears to buy a shovel. If he talked about buying a new car, he made wisecracks about having enough trunk space for her. He knew her height, her approximate weight, and the cubic volume in the trunk for her body.

I was like his ninth attorney, and I gave Kendall a break on legal fees, working on his case for an occasional meal. I kept a tab and he struck off lunches every now and then, scribbling 'comp' in big red letters across the tab. He sweetened the deal, letting me use his outdated all-in-one copier, fax, scanner, and printer at the restaurant.

With all the legal research on the internet and the legal writing performed on my laptop, I had no technical need for an office. I was fine on my own as a solo practitioner, and between Amalia leaving me and now this judge's crazy order, I didn't want to become too isolated.

Kendall and I had rousing discussions at the bar about important political and social issues such as which cell phone carrier had the best coverage and which NFL team had the best chance of going to the Super Bowl. Or about the high profile cases in the news.

He played fantasy football, which had to be the dumbest pastime I have ever seen. It was bad enough to fantasize about your team winning the championship, and watch every game that impacted your team's division. But he fantasized about real players on his imaginary team. Were people really that bored?

We talked about Henry Louis and Kendall's problems with his X. Kendall's belief was that no matter how unfair his life was on earth with his X, there would be a reckoning. This seemed nonsensical. If you want justice, you need to pursue it now, on earth. I explained that religion was like the internet, with different browsers, available to you if you logged in, and only mattering if you let it.

If it helped you—great—but the information was just as unreliable. Immaculate Conception, The Virgin Birth, Rising from the Dead. No one could seriously believe in these things. Apparently, despite our frequent conversations between appointments, Kendall believed in them.

"Kendall," I explained in one of our discussions, "I hope there is justice someday, if not in this life, in the next. Your religion seems rather harsh, wouldn't you say? Think about it legally. Christianity punishes the people who don't believe in it by sentencing them to hell for all eternity. That's a long prison sentence. Eternity. No matter what they did. The exact same punishment for everyone. Simply for not believing. There are no sentencing guidelines in hell. No plea bargains. No possibility of parole. No place in hell for good time. Or ankle bracelets. Or work-release."

Everybody thinks they should have been a lawyer. Or has a friend whose husband or wife worked as a paralegal in some state in some capacity at a law firm. It is rare that a person without a law degree and some trial experience actually knows what he is talking about.

Kendall pontificated about his vast experience in the legal system in light of his prolonged legal problems with his divorce and custody issues. All the false allegations from his wife and the biased court decisions. He had been wronged by his X and the justice system every time.

His time would come, he said, talking about his X again, and he would be vindicated in the afterlife, way up in heaven; if not in this life, in the next.

"There's a legal term for this," Kendall said. "I believe it's called the quid pro crow."

I stared at him, grinning. I couldn't help it. Just like in court, your whole case can succeed or fail on credibility. One wrong word, your credibility is gone forever: quid pro crow as opposed to quid pro quo. After that, he did not mention God again in our discussions.

Philosophically, I appreciated his sentiment about plotting the demise of his X. My relationship with Amalia as an ex was rare. We were still compatible. I wanted the divorce undone. Reversed. As if it never happened.

For Kendall, murdering his ex-wife made a lot of economic sense, especially if you could make it look like an accident.

Lawyers charge by the hour, and the cost of defense for a criminal charge where there is the higher standard of reasonable doubt is conceivably much lower than the massive amounts of fees spent over years and years of petty bickering in a divorce.

Under the Rules of Professional Responsibility for lawyers, even if I took these jokes as threats, these conversations were still privileged under the attorney-client privilege. Turning him in to the authorities was at my discretion. I didn't believe Kendall would harm his X. Custody cases go on for years, and I dismissed his banter as stress from years of ongoing litigation.

Many of my best clients were criminals, and they tended to be dumb enough to get caught over and over again, which is why they were my best clients. A lawyer, like a psychiatrist, only benefits if matters get worse.

I had a real estate client who was a police officer. He carried around a big green beaten-up old flashlight with many nicks and scars on it, suggesting he had successfully gotten away with many violent criminal acts. Sometimes he would hold the flashlight up and grin. "Look!" he'd say. "For every dent and nick and scar there is a story."

I often thought that I would have made a good criminal if only I had started at a younger age. I had seen several episodes of popular TV crime dramas, and I knew enough after committing a violent crime to burn my clothes and throw away my shoes. Lawyers and cops know how to lie in court and they know how to sanitize a crime scene. All careers require training, and the best training is experience. I ruined my career as a possible criminal by following the law.

Crime wasn't what it used to be. Careers as a pick-pocket, for example, or a mugger, have been ruined by technology. People don't carry cash anymore, everyone snaps photos and videos from their cell phones. I'd had experience as a criminal myself.

When I was first married, I quickly learned with Amalia that certain mundane necessities were considered great luxuries in Amalia's country. A phone line, for example. A Whopper and fries at Burger King. An automobile of any kind, even an old Festiva.

One of the rare luxuries was a night out at the movies. Amalia would get dressed up and want to go for a nice meal, too. Once she was dressed up, I had to get dressed up, and a simple night to the movies became a grand event.

Of course, we always disagreed about what movie to see, and we took turns, which meant she chose. She liked the chick flicks but complained if you called the sappy, predictable poorly-acted love story a chick flick. Believe you me, I had a list. I did everything in my power to find a better option. I never had much time for TV. Amalia liked *Sex and the City* reruns, four single girls floozing around the upscale parts of Manhattan, the real one, sleeping indiscriminately with firemen and investment bankers — talking about sex and fashion and shoes. One them was supposedly a lawyer. But she never talked like lawyer. Or thought like a lawyer.

The main character was miraculously able to afford what had to be a three million dollar condominium from her hobby writing a newspaper column about her dating experiences.

What if the four girls in *Sex and the City* were guys? What if Kendall and the regulars at The Overtime had a TV show about his dating experiences with the random women he picked up at the bar? The show would be a bomb.

"Well, I saw her walk into the restaurant, and she was hot. I introduced myself to her at the bar, and we downed some margaritas. I wouldn't kick her out of bed for eating crackers..." I can see Kendall explaining to his sports bar buddies on his hit TV show. "After I boned her, I went to the Army Surplus store and picked out some handsome combat boots... and a new hunting jacket."

I may have criticized the show once or twice when Amalia and I were married.

In one of my outings with Amalia, after going out for a meal, we decided to go to a late movie. When we got to the theater entrance, the teenager collecting tickets briefly left his station, so Amalia and I ducked in without paying. I saw the opportunity and led Amalia past the guard post. Amalia didn't even know what had happened until we were safely seated in the cinema among a crowd of paying moviegoers.

There was a thrill in committing this crime, and an additional thrill in Amalia's lack of complicity. Like the felon who talks his girlfriend into driving him to the bank for an errand, leaves her waiting in the car while he robs the bank, and forces his girl into the awkward unfortunate position of getaway driver and co-conspirator. But the thrill soon wore off. I sat in the back row during the entire movie, shaking, staring at the aisle, waiting for SWAT. After the movie, I left twelve dollars for the two tickets under the seat to reimburse the theater.

If I had the protracted domestic legal problems that Kendall had, I could see myself planning and executing a brilliant plan to kill Amalia.

The detailed planning was not the problem. Nor was covering up the evidence. The getaway from the crime scene could be well-planned with numerous alternatives in place if the job didn't work out exactly as anticipated.

Even if I succeeded in some crazy scheme, I could also see myself being questioned by the police. And the husband is always the first one they interrogate, especially in a case where there was a divorce. Instead of simply stoically asking the police for a lawyer as I advise my own clients, I'm afraid I would seem too interested in the investigation and act like a suspect in ways only a police detective would surmise.

Or worse (and more likely based on my experience in the movie theater), I would simply break down and bawl out a confession from the back of the police car.

And no joke, I really did want to get back with Amalia.

15

Every day I looked at the same dull menu and ordered the same thing. Kendall made a mean Reuben. I had tried other entrees — Kendall was always inventing new specials, spicing the food up to keep up with trends — but I was pretty happy with my sandwich and a basket of fries on the side. Amalia would have had me order something healthier, like a salad. A salad always left me hungry. She always knew when I cheated on my diet, another one of her talents. I never found out how she knew.

The waitress at The Overtime was a young, black-haired girl, bright, friendly, wide beautiful eyes. 'Woman,' I should say. 'Female.' 'Chick' was the word from my day, banned now in civilized circles. (Like in my grandfather's day, blacks were called 'coloreds'; that would be a huge scandal today.)

Her name was Cora. And she looked like a Cora, too. She had a nametag which she refused to wear but she kept it and fiddled with it in the pocket of her uniform. She was obviously a student. She kept a backpack filled with books and her tablet by her waitress station, pulling out her homework when business was slow.

She had a nose ring and I could only imagine what other

piercings. In her neat red uniform, she looked barely half my age. I could not tell exactly. Caught up in the coolness of her youth, her breasts slipping and sliding beneath her t-shirt like hockey pucks every time she moved.

She looked like she would be fun to be around. I missed the fun I used to have with Amalia. The music was better, the food was better, the beer was better, and the sex was better when I was young.

Cora always smiled at me. Whether it was coffee with a client or a full-blown meal, I gave her a generous tip.

I had never cheated on Amalia except for the diet, not even when she went out of town. Naturally, I had thought about it. I had not dated since the divorce. You'd think a successful attorney like me with a killer suit and an old TV ad would have an easy time finding women. You'd think it would be raining pussy. But I was out of touch with the dating scene since I got married. I couldn't see myself cruising the bars like a twenty-four-year-old.

I had dated a number of women before I married Amalia, and I had found them on the internet even while I was married. I had even sold houses to some of my ex-girlfriends. I used to keep track of these women, just in case. Some of them were on my mailing list. I remembered them as young, as they were back then. I naturally assumed, without really thinking about it, that if Amalia went home to Argentina, each woman would want to pick up the slack and take up where we left off when I married Amalia. That was my grand plan.

When Amalia was out of town, I would have weeks to myself alone at the Three Lakes House, and I frequently conjured up scenarios reliving the sexual freedom of single life.

Not at the house, mind you; Amalia was smart and I was

bound to get caught.

There were small mountain resort towns where we could blend in with the tourists and we wouldn't be recognized. I figured since we had gone out before I married, it wasn't really cheating.

The problem was many of my clients were fix-and-flippers or land developers who knew Amalia. I could easily run into them in a resort where they might have a project going.

There was a town off the Interstate out east with nothing but a big truck stop called the Moccasin, a rundown old motel, and a raucous live country music bar. I imagined a night or two of taking one of these women—it didn't matter which one—for drinks at the music bar and making love to her in the motel room with red shag carpet and matching polyester sheets and pillows, waking up with her in my arms and having breakfast at the truck stop, hanging out in the town until the bar opened up again and then meeting up with another one. This town was on the plains; with no water supply for new development and no trees, it has no appeal to a developer, and no one, not my friends, not my fellow attorneys, not Amalia's friends would ever go there. I could cheat on Amalia there easily and not be recognized. Each time the opportunity arose—each time Amalia went back home for a week or two or a month, even—I chickened out and then lost interest. I didn't think about it.

When Amalia went out of town, instead of pursuing the women on my list, I missed her; I spent my whole time working, watching old *Sex and the City* and *Project Runway* reruns, and waiting for her phone calls from Argentina. In my head, I always found my way back to Amalia.

Amalia had played hard to get, not giving in until we were

married. Exotic, wild and intense, it was like doing a jaguar.

Now that I was single again, I thought about joining one of these internet dating sites. Or pursuing these hot young law clerks, court reporters, and paralegals. But I wasn't ready. My brain was locked into Amalia.

I didn't want the divorce and I didn't want to start over with someone else. I looked well-fed, some would say, pleasantly plump; I needed some time at the gym to get myself into a presentable physical condition. That could take years. And who has the time for relationships? I was preoccupied with this crazy order to write a book and my pressing law appointments.

Of course, this was a problem. I didn't mind being alone, but I didn't really like it. Sometimes my smart phone was like my only friend. At first I was reluctant to buy one; now I don't know how I ever lived without it. It coos at me. It listens to me. I have separation anxiety if I don't carry it with me. And I check it constantly, to see if someone has texted or emailed me.

The voice on the smart phone—if only I could program it to speak in broken English with a Spanish accent.

Touching myself (again) as I thought of Amalia or one of my female clients. Still hoping to get back with Amalia.

When I looked at Kendall's problems with his X and thought about my own divorce—thank God Amalia and didn't have children. His X kept a notebook of Kendall's parenting time. The time of the pick-ups and drop-offs, how Henry Louis was dressed, his disposition, etc. If Kendall was two minutes late picking up Henry Louis for his visitation, she would cancel his parenting time. Once, when Kendall's car broke down, and he was forty minutes late in returning Henry Louis, she tried to have him arrested for false imprisonment and kidnapping. Another time she broke down her own door after a parenting exchange, filed a police report accusing Kendall of domestic violence, had him charged with criminal trespass, vandalism, and property damage. She even forced him to go through the risk, stress, and expense of a five-day jury trial in which he was acquitted.

In the last incident, she even got a restraining order against him, prohibited him from working at his own restaurant for ten days. Another crazy judge's order. Go figure; she didn't even work at The Overtime anymore.

The child was obviously gifted (like her), but he failed the qualifying entrance examine for the Gifted and Talented Program. She insisted on holding Henry Louis back a year so he would be the oldest, strongest, and smartest in his class. Next time — goddamn it — he would pass.

Mom enrolled Henry Louis in kindergarten in the school in her neighborhood on her parenting time — Monday, Wednesday, and Friday — without Dad's consent. Henry Louis liked his school, the jungle gym on the playground, his new teacher, was involved in soccer, and made new friends.

On his parenting time, Tuesday and Thursday, Dad enrolled Henry Louis in first grade in the school in his neighborhood a few miles away — without Mom's consent. Henry Louis liked this school also, the jungle gym on the playground, his new teacher, was involved in soccer, and made new friends.

This went on for months until Judge Tezak sorted it out. No wonder Kendall joked about killing her.

Some couples should be banned from breeding. All the money these parents spent on custody disputes, the child could have gone to Yale.

16

My decision to simply accept the order left me with some relief from the shock the order originally gave me. I began to think in more detail about the court-ordered book, the guidebook, I sometimes called it. I was disgraced, and the Order put me on diversion. One thing that made me feel better about my decision — the lack of success of my friends from law school. None of my friends from law school had exactly thrived, as far as I could tell, and I wasted some time I could have been writing the book internetting some of these esteemed colleagues.

My daily law practice was consumed with making and responding to phone calls, conducting initial consultations at The Overtime, sending emails and writing motions, interviewing witnesses and investigating the facts of each case, doing legal research, preparing for court appearances, sending out and trying to collect bills, admittedly erratically. Some of the calls to my practice were from people who obviously couldn't afford an attorney asking for free legal advice.

I never got used to this. Strangers calling me with a question or two. I would never call a CPA to ask a free question or two about my taxes, and I would expect any decent professional to at least set up an appointment before wasting his or her time. Does Dairy Queen give out free Blizzards? Why should my time be free?

I usually tried to help anyway. The purpose of taking the phone call was to set up the free initial consultation. I could avoid the entire meeting if I answered their questions, even though I was opening myself to liability for giving legal advice without having been officially retained and without investigating the facts of the case.

Others calls were from bill collectors or phone solicitations. I never gave to charities because I was short on money myself. Besides, most charities keep most, if not all, of the money that they received in donations. If I wanted to help the homeless, for example, I would go down and help by dishing out soup at the homeless shelter. Amalia and I talked about doing that. We never made it, though.

One caller who was soliciting was kind enough to offer me a credit card—a generous offer for a man with no money, a beater car, living in a HUD house. The banks charge more to the less fortunate people who need the money. The interest rate on the credit card was 36 percent. Thanks but no thanks.

All the law appointments started with a free initial consultation that required a face-to-face meeting. I instructed the potential client to bring all of his documents and his checkbook, in case he wanted to retain me. You would think this would be implied.

I always wore my suit for the first interview to compensate for not having an office. Sometimes I would lose them when I suggested an initial meeting at The Overtime. I understand this; the appearance of professionalism is what they are expecting.

Sometimes I would explain I was looking for new office space, which since I used to have an office, could have been true.

If a prospective client missed an appointment, was late for the appointment, was not well organized, or if I didn't think I could truly help, I did not take the case. As a lawyer, I am selling my time, and in my mind, nothing is worse or more insulting than being late.

Another rule: no drinking at The Overtime. I liked to make a professional appearance.

When I first got my real estate license, I drove around with a case of beer while my prospective buyers, also in their twenties, downed the beers listening to bootleg Tom Waits cassettes and looking at houses. I carried the cassettes in an old vegetable crate in the back seat. We all got a little wasted and we usually ended up at a bar in Cherry Creek called the Cricket. This was illegal. Arguably.

At the free initial consultation, I made the prospective clients fill out a questionnaire that requested their income, contact information, and address.

This information allowed me to figure out if they could really afford me. It's something to always ask about. Not only if they had the money, but if they could get the money from someone else.

My time, concern, and expertise, that's what I sell. Lawyers charge for their time, and the amount of time depends on the attitude of the litigant or the attorneys, whether they want to settle or run up the fees. That is the truth about the practice of law: it's not what's true that matters, not what is right, but what you can prove, and how much money you want to spend proving it.

I accepted a divorce where the parties fought over a golden

retriever. A dog is treated as personal property; there is no dog child support or dog parenting time. On the other hand, parenting plans for children are based on legal and equitable factors and what the court determines is best for the child. There is no Best Interests of the Puppy standard, or in this case, The Best Interests of the Golden Retriever. It was quite a dilemma. You can't give one person the head of the dog, the other the rump.

Some judges side with the woman in a case, some with the man. Judges are human, and that's how it is sometimes. I know what Amalia would say about this case. I could hear her discussing the case in my head.

You'd think Amalia would automatically side with the woman. Maybe on a child custody case. But no. Not on a dog case. I knew how she thought from previous cases.

"It's just a dog," I could hear her say. "Tell the judge you're sorry for wasting his time. Tell the judge to pick one --- the husbands or the wife, it doesn't matter. Whoever gets the dog, pays half for another dog. The case is over, case closed. "

I researched precedent. Copied and organized my exhibits. I worked up my questions for trial and for cross examination. My opening and my closing. I even hired a dog expert as a rebuttal witness to the wife's dog expert.

My client had paid for the purchase of the dog. His X had cared for the dog and paid the vet bills, which totaled more than the dog cost. He walked the dog in the morning. She walked the dog in the evening. It was a tough case. He said, she said.

The morning before the hearing, the dog died.

Normally, this would be the end of the dispute. Except the wife requested to see the dog's carcass. This became a problem because (and I didn't know this at the time) the dog did not really die. So my client studied up on poisons and bought rat poison to really kill the dog this time, but he just couldn't do it. At the next hearing, he testified the dog made a miraculous medical recovery, and the dog was fine. The wife was so relieved that the dog survived, she gave him custody.

I was retained by a woman on a custody dispute... of a child this time. At the final hearing, the husband claimed to be a better parent because he was a Methodist. He attended church frequently. Volunteered with the youth basketball team. I objected to this whole line of questioning.

"Nothing against the Mighty Methodists," I declared. "I'm sure there are a few Catholics and Presbyterians who disagree. And what about the Unitarians? Unitarians believe in everything."

The judge sided with me. A judge can't favor one religion over another, he just can't. I called that the 'Mighty Methodist Case.'

Justice rolled!

17

I met with a prospective client, a woman named Melanie Hall, over a dispute with her neighborhood homeowner's association. She lived in an older subdivision of starter homes called The Meadows II. She was about fifteen years younger than me, single, and attractive. She showed me pictures of her home which she had redone.

During the initial interview, I told war stories about my experiences litigating against homeowner's associations. These stories add to my credibility. I advised her to always bring her own witness with her to the HOA meetings, if she went, because board members and adverse witnesses lie, witnesses lie all the time.

As I told her a few of the stories, I couldn't help but wonder that after I won her case, what it would be like to go to a barbeque at Melanie's on her new redwood deck. She would invite her neighbors, some of them also disgruntled with the Homeowners Association, and there would be other cases. She would introduce me as her lawyer, The Superman Slayer, the one who beat the HOA. And later in the evening, after the guests left, we would make love under her colorful comforter in her bed in her big master that had been two smaller rooms before she renovated the property. Things like this never happened to me.

Despite many of the homes in the area being in much worse condition, the Homeowners Association demanded she paint the exterior of her home. The paint job was only two-years-old, was an approved color, but was done without the HOA's approval. She showed me some photos of her home before she painted it, her home now, and several of the homes of her neighbors, and it looked better than most of them.

She lived with her dog. She flashed a photo of a little curly-haired dog that looked like a mop with legs; it looked like a tribble. What with the responsibility of owning a dog, she couldn't afford to repaint the house at the whim of the HOA. She could barely afford to stay current in her monthly dues, and her mother lent her money to retain a lawyer.

The dog was a mix between a teacup poodle and a teaspoon Shih-Tzu. A 'Shitz-Doodle.' That's how she pronounced it. At first I thought the Shitz-Doodle was made up. It sounded made up— like a rabbit-bat. I looked it up on the Google. No, it was a real breed. I guess people were so bored that they had to create new breeds of goofy looking dogs.

She called the dog 'Jewel,' after the world-famous singer, or perhaps (I thought as a lawyer) after the last name of the falsely accused person of interest in the Atlanta Olympic Park bombings.

I wrote the HOA a letter, explaining the house complied with the restrictive covenants. I hoped that would be the end of it. The letter was easy and I couldn't charge her much of anything.

A lot of my practice is drafting letters, motions, and briefs which I simply plagiarize either from past work or from opposing counsel in old cases, especially after all these years. Nothing wrong with that. There are no copyright issues in the practice of law. In fact, it's flattering if someone steals your work. You don't fix something that's not broken.

18

Along with my law practice, I still maintained my real estate broker's license. I sold houses through my company, Wyn Realty, which was just me as the broker. With real estate, you really don't need an office. You show houses, you write offers at a restaurant, or you list houses and fill out the paperwork at the seller's home. The closings, for the most part, occur at the title company.

Most of my real estate clients were from the past. I had not sold so many houses lately, because of the market and because I lost contact with most of my 'sphere.' Something over time a few advertising mailings, refrigerator magnets, and lunches probably could have cured. Or farming, which is when you inundate a neighborhood with your free ice scrapers and flyers until — out of pity — people break down and list their houses with you.

The first time I lost a bunch of my clients was when I married Amalia. Because she was South American, many of my real estate clients didn't like her. Even though Amalia was from a wealthy family, they naturally assumed I had married the maid. Before I was married, I would hang out with my real estate clients, most of whom were friends, trying to get referrals; once I met Amalia, I decided to spend more time with my wife. And after she answered the phone a few times when people called and asked her if she was indeed the maid, she began to isolate me. No more afternoon barbeques or talk of tax-deductible holiday trips with clients to Vail or Deadwood or Lake Powell.

The second time I lost them — when we decided to stop trying to have children. Once my clients had children, the conversations quickly changed from the Super Bowl to Pee Wee Football, from parties at rock concerts to tickets to Barney.

The third time was after my divorce. When you divide your property, you also divide your friends.

My HUD house was up for sale, which distracted me from working on the book, practicing law, and selling homes. It subjected me to rude, unannounced intrusions by real estate brokers. The brokers all had a key to the lockboxes on the government houses, and they could appear without notice. The lockboxes were uniform, and one key gave you access to every HUD home.

I took the lockbox off the home temporarily so I could pretend to be showing the home also if a showing occurred. I usually left the home during normal showing hours, and when I returned, I often found real estate cards left on the kitchen counter. I was gone most days, anyway, but I always had to duck out if a showing occurred.

You would think there would be more cross-over from the law practice to the real estate business and vice versa. A real estate broker shows houses and essentially practices law without a license --- filling out the approved forms. The two professions are similar, but the business cultures are different.

The law clients think that because I am a lawyer, I am too busy to show them houses if they need a broker. They want a real go-getter as a real estate broker, not a broker/lawyer bogged down with motions deadlines, drafting jury instructions, conducting depositions, and preparing for and attending court appearances. They simply don't see me as a broker. I can go to court for a year and against all odds save them from a wrongful conviction. When they buy a home, they go through their neighborhood realtor, because he was nice once, had given them a refrigerator magnet, and said hello.

Similarly, the real estate clients, if they need a lawyer, don't want me as their lawyer. They usually want a real go-getter as a lawyer, not a lawyer/broker who is bogged down by a bunch of appointments showing houses, writing offers and counteroffers, holding open houses and attending closings.

The problem with houses in general: men design houses, but women select them. Men conceive, create, and construct them; women are the ultimate buyers of houses with features pragmatically engineered and designed by men.

Death is good for real estate. So is divorce. So is bankruptcy. If your cousin dies in a terrible automobile accident, great, his house goes on the market. If you lose your job or your wife leaves you, yippee! You will have to move. That is why as a real estate broker, I tend to be more upbeat than as a lawyer. There will always be some new disaster that will result in a motivated buyer or seller.

With that in mind, I always figure I can find a buyer a home, and if one home doesn't work out for them, there will be another. Unlike the practice of law, where the results of a case can be permanent and hard to overturn.

Oh, and never buy a house without letting your wife see it first. If you don't let your wife view the home, your wife will mention it every time there is a plumbing leak, a squeaky door,

even a burnt out light-bulb. And you will never ever again get...
well... you know...

Most of my buyers preferred to drive their own cars when I showed houses, making it easy for me. Especially buyers with families. Maybe it was my stylish Festiva. Maybe it was because I had a habit of playing with my phone as I drove, sometimes blowing through stop signs, and that made them nervous.

(No need to transfer the car seats, honey. Just as well, I lacked gas money.)

As I showed houses, I tried to personalize the house-hunting experience. I encouraged buyers to give the houses nicknames — practice for making the big decision. Nicknames are important. If a home is not named, it is not memorable, and you tend to empty it out of your mind. But if the home is darling, and the nickname is darling, it tends to make the buyers more comfortable; it tends to make the buyers fall in love with the house.

Nicknames such as The Green House for the house with green carpet; The Honey Bee House for the house with yellow siding and black trim. The Dog House for the house with the cute dog. Cute dog not included. Then I would have my clients rank them.

A hard decision, buying a home. A housing purchase is always part emotion and part financial. I never pressured buyers to buy. When the house-hunting couple sat down in the family room during the second or third showing, stretched out on the sofa to talk about the house, I knew it was time to shut up, to let them work out the details between them; that is when I knew they were ready to make an offer.

19

The practice of law was much more complicated than the real estate business and filled with drama. I took a case where a high school student was jumped by some bullies from the football team. My client was walking down the hall, listening to tunes on his iPod when several football players jumped him. There was a big row in the hallway. The entire incident was caught on the school's surveillance camera.

Although my client was the victim of this vicious attack, he was the one who was expelled from school, he was the one criminally charged. Worse, he had just turned 18 so he was charged as an adult.

The prosecutor didn't want to charge the football players because, God forbid, it would hurt their chances for college scholarships. I went down to the Algonquin County Court for a court date, a brief meeting with the DA and a short appearance before the judge.

The case was commenced B.O. which meant Before Judge Solomon's Order. That's how I began to categorize my cases. Before the Order, I was unfettered with worry about my law license; I was not scrutinized, free to take whatever cases and make whatever silly arguments I wanted.

After the Order, I had to be careful. There are dozens and dozens of rules that are always changing, and lawyers have the duty to keep up with the rules. I have never heard of a lawyer being excused from a rule for simply not knowing about it, and the Disciplinary Committee was now potentially watching every move I made.

Once you are in their sights, they will examine you more closely and find other rules you may have violated. Add additional charges against you.

I always showed up early for court, in case the matter was moved to another division. This gave me time to check in with the clerk, review my file again, exchange exhibits, talk to my client or to opposing counsel. I sometimes skipped lunch before going to court, especially if I was meeting with the prosecutor. This put me in a more disagreeable mood.

In a civil case, the judge will rule against you in default if you don't appear within twenty minutes of when your case is called. Some judges don't wait at all; if you're not there when they call your case, they start without you.

In a criminal case, there's no default, the judge simply issues a warrant. An FTA. Which means Failure to Appear. This means there's a warrant out for your arrest, and the police are supposed to be out looking for you; they rarely do. But if the police ever stumble upon you, say, for example, on a routine traffic stop, the police will take you straight to jail.

On the way to the courtroom to meet my high school student client and his mother, I had to pass through security, which was like taking an international flight. I stood in line with all the prospective jurors, witnesses, and my fellow attorneys, removed my shoes, handed over my belt, my keys, and my phone. I felt a certain loss of dignity as I walked through holding up my pants from falling down.

The DAs and court employees had official badges and were waved on through. This made no sense to me. You had security for everyone, or don't have security. Like a DA or a janitor wasn't just as likely — if not more likely — to bring a gun or plant a bomb in the courtroom. Police submitted my briefcase to an x-ray machine. A police officer had me raise my arms, and he patted me down, just in case.

The way I see it, like any business, a law degree is worth what it brings in revenue. If it wasn't for the divorce, I could net a hundred-fifty thousand dollars a year, and if you are going to work for another fifteen years, well, do the math; no matter how frustrating the practice can be, no matter how upset I was over Judge Solomon's order, I am not going to go off the deep end soon.

After I gathered my shoes, my keys, my belt, and my briefcase, the police officer in security gave me this intense stare. He was watching me. Like he was about to arrest me.

He followed me into the elevator. He stood next to me and kept staring, his badge shining, mumbling into his walkie-talkie, his black pistol in a holster by his side. I was standing right next to him and could have simply grabbed his shiny black weapon. I wondered if it was loaded. He smelled like sweat and cigarettes. He did not say a word to me. When I exited the elevator, he followed me down the hallway to Courtroom Four. I walked faster, he walked faster; I slowed down to look at my phone, he slowed down, kind of lingering behind me. Was this a coincidence? He mumbled something again into his walkie-talkie. Finally, in the hallway by the courtroom, he tapped me on the shoulder.

What had I done? Silence.

"Did you win, Wyn?" he asked, finally, with a goofy smile.

There he stood. In front of me. Beaming. He seemed impressed by his own lack of originality. A moment of recognition of my inglorious past. I thought he was going to ask for my autograph. Although he had spooked me a little with his gun and badge, I didn't want to disappoint him. I had to say something witty here.

"I'm flattered you remember those TV commercials," I replied. "Do you remember Green Stamps, too?"

This was the best I could do.

A voice mumbled something to the police officer through his walkie-talkie.

"Just doing my job, sir," he said. "Carry on."

I have to admit, it was nice to have fans like a rock band; except my followers had way better jobs and much nicer vans.

20

The first thing I did before court was check the docket—the pages and pages of scheduled hearings posted on the wall outside the courtroom. That makes the case real, and my presence official. I looked for my case with my name as counsel of record and the estimated amount of time allotted for the hearing. All of these cases were set for the same time. If you ever wondered how ten matters can be scheduled for one hour at the same time, I always wondered that, too. The court system assumes most of the cases will settle.

After I found my case, I looked for names of attorneys I had done cases with before, my old attorney, Traffic Jack, or maybe lawyers I knew from law school.

I thought I saw Donald Douglas Trickey's name on the docket, the lawyer who had sabotaged my real estate deal. I've lost plenty of cases over the years, but I can count on the fingers of one hand the number of real estate deals that failed at the closing table, especially those that failed for no reason. I looked around the courtroom. If Trickey was there, I didn't see him.

While I was looking for my client, I saw people walk by me in the hallway. Some of them were litigants or witnesses, others were jurors.

It is amazing how many people go to court in t-shirts and tennis shoes. They bring their children because they can't afford a babysitter... like they are on their way to the Laundromat or running an errand. This is a mistake when you stand in front of a judge. Your first impression may be your only impression. Court is all about appearances.

If you ever want to mess up a judge's trial, simply talk to an innocent juror in the hallway during lunch or at a trial break. Jurors are supposed to be pure, listening only to the judge's instructions and the evidence allowed by the judge at trial. Not the internet. Not the newspapers. Not casual conversations with strangers in the hallway.

Talk to a juror about your case, about the weather, about anything. The juror will have to report it to the judge, and the case could end in a mistrial.

I found my client and his mom and I checked in with the clerk, a friendly young woman with big green eyes and striking orange hair. She sat in front of the courtroom behind her computer screen with a stack of court files next to her on the desk.

I am always nice to the clerks because the judges often ask them for their opinions, and if you need a clerk to put your case on the top of her stack of files, it is important to have this relationship. In fact, many of the clerks are law students or lawyers, just out of law school.

After talking to the clerk about her future plans as a lawyer, I would sit in the first row in the front of the courtroom. Just to be seen. My client and his mom sat a row or two behind me.

In a civil docket, the collection attorneys gather in the back of the courtroom and try to make deals with the people they've summoned. In a criminal docket, the DAs hold their pre-trial conferences, one by one, with the defendants or their lawyers. All the litigants check in with the clerk and the lawyers and the defendants negotiate while court is going on for other cases.

Prosecutors put people in jail. Guilty or not. That's their job; that's what they do. If there is any evidence at all to support the criminal charge, they pursue it. Reputation and saving face are way more important than justice. In their world, the crumpled-up Constitution and the Rules of Evidence are designed to help the criminals go free. Trials are merely a technicality. If the guy did it — he did it; let's go straight to sentencing. And if he is innocent, he no doubt did something else.

Defense attorneys get criminals off. Guilty or not. That's their job; that's what they do. The same principle in reverse. Trials are the only thing that protects the citizen from unfair governmental prosecution. In their world, the Constitution and the Rules of Evidence protect everyone from government bullying, even if a person committed a horrible crime. The difference between a prosecutor and a public defender is not just the job, it's the philosophy.

My job as the defense attorney is to convince the prosecuting attorney he doesn't have much of a case. File motions, set up hearings, request discovery, bog him down until he wants to give me a deal. Negotiate the charges down to something the client can live with. Sort through the menu of lesser charges, find one that won't affect their job or ability to go back to school. Keep it up until the deal sweetens.

The judge calls the cases as they are ready to be heard. He usually first calls the in-custody defendants, in their orange jumpsuits and restraints, being transported by the sheriff's escort fresh from a night or two in jail. Next the Court calls the defendants who require interpreters. Then as a courtesy, the judge will call cases of parties with private attorneys.

My iPod client was—admittedly and understandably—not the type of student the school district wanted to attend that school. Although the school was a public school in one of the poorer suburbs, it had the highest academic standards, and the school was trying to elevate its academic reputation. After all, my client had Cs and worse, he didn't play sports.

Criminal law is a lot like negotiating a real estate deal, though instead of arguing about the value of the new carpet in a home you are trying to sell, the renovated kitchen, or the mountain view, you talk about the elements of the crime, the facts of the case, and mitigating circumstances.

I began to think that if these students in this case randomly attacked my client in the hallway, they didn't deserve college scholarships. The court system is all about being held accountable.

If I robbed a bank, it wouldn't be a defense to say please don't arrest me, I will lose my law license. If you don't want to lose your license, don't rob the bank. If you want a college scholarship, don't mug other students in the hallway.

When I met with the DA, I reviewed the file; I had already interviewed my client and heard his version of events. I had read the police report and the charging document, pulled out the elements of the charges, the legal precedent and my client's defenses. Sometimes your greatest weapon is showing up with the most likely version of the facts and the correct legal precedent.

That's plan A. You are right and they are wrong, and you get in their face. If that doesn't work, there is always Plan B—Grovel. Show your client is worth saving. Beg for a deal. If your facts are no good and they can prove their case, you can always bluff them.

If that doesn't succeed at first, drag it out. Make them do the work. When you go to court, you simply hope for a break or that common sense sets in.

Other times, no matter how right you are, no matter what you do, how prepared you are, how clever or correct you are, you simply lose. Not even Johnny Cochran up in heaven can help you.

In reviewing the file, something was not right in this case. My client was attacked in the hallway; he was the victim. I looked through the file at the witness statements. All the statements were in the same handwriting. They started the same way, with the same phrasing: "I was walking down the hallway, minding my own business when…"

Contrary to what you might think, cases aren't usually won or lost on questionable arguments or clever court antics. Cases are won or lost on tiny little details like these.

Upon further inquiry, all of the statements were written by the same person—the high school football coach—and he wasn't even present at the incident. I could hear Amalia in my head: "Tell the judge to dismiss the case. Put them all in jail or let them all go free. All or none. That's what you say to the judge. "

Unconscionable. Unforgivable. Egregious.

That's what I told the DA and he reluctantly agreed. Those college football scholarships were far more important than a petty misunderstanding in the hallway.

"Thank you," the mother said. "I'm so relieved."

My client shook my hand.

"Good luck in school," I said. I would have made an excellent dad.

Case dismissed. Justice reprieved.

21

Although I had (finally) resigned myself to complying with Judge Solomon's order, that did not make it less unjust. I thought there must be some way to comply with the order and still express my disappointment.

The order gave a length minimum of sixty-five thousand words, a brief description of the subject — the dignity and integrity of the legal system — but no other critical requirements.

I began writing down random notes — a few pointers and rules — as an outline for the guidebook. Writing them on napkins at The Overtime or on the backs of envelopes. In a notebook, which I placed in a file like any other case. My thoughts and ideas about what I wanted to say and still be in full compliance with both the language and the spirit of Judge Solomon's order. Words or parts of words, barely legible, that I would no doubt struggle to decipher later.

First rule, before even stepping foot in a courtroom, hire me. Hire an attorney familiar with the court and with this type of law. If you don't you will probably lose, because you do not know the rules, and lawyers have studied the rules. You are bound by the rules even if you do not hire a lawyer.

Second rule, read the rules. In the field of law, there are rules for everything. Some judges are really picky. Come prepared when you go to court. Bring four copies of every exhibit: one for you, one for the other side, one for the judge, and one for the witness on the stand. The Plaintiff's exhibits are marked with numbers, Defendant's letters.

Do not leave your evidence in your apartment or your truck. If you do, you are out of luck.

When you go to court, always dress well. Turn off your cell phone. Toss out your Slurpee and your scone.

You need to be devoid of personality when you address the judge. The best lawyers are grey. Talk to the judge simply, like you are talking to a child. No matter how boring or predictable, never interrupt a judge.

Be reasonable. Try and think like a judge would think. Never correct a judge's grammar or pronunciation. Judges don't like it. You need to learn when to speak and when to listen and shut up.

Third rule, the judge can make jokes, but you can't. I once lost a case because my client joked she wanted a million dollars at a deposition for a low-end case. A million dollars! At the trial in front of a jury, opposing counsel quoted and repeated it a dozen times.

I heard of one lawyer who defended a female client from a charge of prostitution; he jokingly asked the arresting officer if he'd take $500 to forget the incident, and he was suspended from the practice of law for three years.

Direct examination of a witness is open-ended questions. Cross examination is yes-and-no questions. Never ask a question unless you know how the witness will answer.

And the judges sometimes speak in code. If you object to a question and the judge says, "I'll give it the weight it deserves," it means the judge knows it is nonsense but is going to allow the testimony anyway, and then ignore it.

Next rule. Bring a copy of any precedent so the judge doesn't have to look it up. The easier you make it for the judge, the better. Assume the judge knows nothing about the case. That is likely to be true. The judge has many, many cases, and he is not sitting alone in his chambers, waiting for a case to work on, excited by the very next motion that you or your lawyer may have filed.

Assume the witnesses against you will lie. They will. Even with the best facts, your chances of winning at trial are fifty/fifty. The police are not your friends. And they can trick you, too.

They really will use whatever you say against you in a court of law.

If you are being interviewed, never ask a cop or a DA if you need a lawyer. They will always say no, because if you ask for a lawyer they can no longer question you.

Look, if your car breaks down, you need a mechanic. If you are dragged into the legal system, you need a lawyer. The cops and prosecutors believe everyone is breaking the law. It is a question of how much and whether it is worth their time to prove it. They get a little Brownie point for every crime they solve and every case they close.

Another consideration while testifying in court: if you answer a question with a "yes," don't shake your head "no."

Next rule, never take legal advice from paralegals, internet chat rooms, home inspectors, bartenders, Uber drivers, property managers, prosecutors, or opposing counsel. Or anyone without a massive student loan. Don't take legal advice from country music songs.

Did I mention rule number one? Hire me.

Another rule: never go to court drunk. Judges don't like it. You would think this was obvious, but it is not obvious to some. Never drive yourself to court if your driver's license is suspended.

This is illegal. Most likely.

22

As a way to subvert the order, I began to research cases similar to mine, and I found a case where a famous TV actress was given a big advance and two years to write her autobiography. While we were both required to write, her case was different from mine because it was a contract between her and her publisher for cash, and not a disciplinary proceeding as punishment with more trouble to come if I did not complete it.

Although the actress was hot, her show was not; it was cancelled by the network, and the publisher lost interest in the project. When her time to turn in the book ran out, the publisher wanted either the book or a refund of the advance.

But the actress had already spent the big advance and hadn't even started the book. She hired a lawyer and submitted the phone book. Her lawyer maintained that under the terms of the contract that there was no requirement that the book be of a certain quality, and the phone book met the length requirements. This resulted in a huge lawsuit over the ordinary meaning of the language of her book contract.

If it worked for the actress, it could work for me. I could submit the Yellow Pages — if they still made them. Let the judge's fingers do the walking.

My other thought—I could submit a 'brief' but 'appealing' book of recipes. This certainly would be in technical compliance with the order. Although I rarely cooked, Amalia kept her family recipes in the kitchen drawer in the Three Lakes house.

I could easily borrow them, have them translated. Maybe even ask Amalia to prepare the dishes and submit photos along with the recipes—in both English and Spanish. The book would be beautiful and I could move on.

She would be flattered if I used her native recipes. Amalia had repeatedly assured me that everything was better in South America. As she would point out, better culture, better holidays, better music. Better pizza, better coffee, better steakhouses, and better weather. Apparently, based on her experience with the death of one of her great aunts, better funerals, too. From what I gathered, her country even had better diseases. More fashionable shoes. Much better recipes. A gourmet mixture of European and native American food... the Italy of South America. As compared to the fine culinary creations of a Colonel Sanders or a Ray Kroc.

Although submitting the phone book or the recipes would be amusing—and it would serve the judge right—it would likely lead to more sanctions. Whenever I contemplated doing something really, really clever, and maybe even devious, it turned out later to be stupid. I remembered Judge Solomon and his scowl.

He had called me 'Counselor.' I could still hear the word in his own voice in my head. Wham! Ouch. Stinging me like a bee. A lawyer is an 'attorney and counselor' at law. A judge only calls you 'counselor' if you are in real trouble. After that, I dropped the idea of the phone book or the recipes.

23

Another rule to include in the book: Know the judge, or at least know something about the judges you go in front of. Most proceedings are open, and you can learn from observing the demeanor of the judge on the case. You can see what arguments impress him and what arguments flounder, and possibly hear arguments on cases with facts similar to yours.

I took a new DUI case in front of another nutty judge, Judge Frost. Cold as Frost. And yes, that was his real name. He had a reputation for being hard-nosed, if not unfair. After his experience representing banks in a large firm, Frost had been a judge in the lower county court, presiding over evictions, collection cases, and restraining orders — cases without lawyers.

I had a run-in with this judge several years before. Judge Frost had set a pre-trial conference with the prosecutor on a criminal case at 2 p.m. but the DAs didn't show up at the appointed time. I waited with the defendant (and all the defendants) until 2:20.

I figured if my client had been twenty minutes late, a warrant would be issued against him. If I didn't appear, the court could find me in contempt. It was not fair that the DA could be this tardy. I tried to get the case dismissed for the late appearance of the DA.

My motion was denied. Instead of exacting an apology or an explanation from the DA, Judge Frost explained that the DAs were very very busy, their time (as opposed to mine) was extremely valuable.

As I sat in the courtroom waiting for my case to be called, I observed Judge Frost making his questionable and irrational rulings once again.

In one case, a man who represented himself got behind in his credit card payments. He was a Latino and struggled with his English.

A collection attorney bought the debt, sued him, and with very little effort got a judgment against him.

I recognized the collection attorney's name --- it was the homeowner's association attorney from Melanie's case. We had written letters back and forth, and nothing had happened on the case. Some cases are dormant for a while or never develop into anything; others, the attorneys churn when they need to generate fees.

To collect on the debt, the collection attorney sent this defendant discovery requests about his finances, which he was required to answer. Instead of answering the requests, he got contributions from his friends and family members – what Amalia called a pasanaku – and simply paid the debt.

The debt was satisfied, the case was dismissed, the collection company was satisfied. Even after the dismissal, Judge Frost required him to appear in court and threatened to put him in jail for contempt for failing to respond to the initial discovery requests, which were now moot. The collection company's attorneys did not even appear at the hearing.

"I don't understand why am I in the court," the poor confused defendant said.

"I cannot give you legal advice," Judge Frost scolded. "I will tell you for the third time. You are here to explain why you did not answer the discovery questions about the judgment. I gave you specific discovery orders. Even though the case has been dismissed, you are here to explain why you have refused to follow my orders."

"But I paid the bill. I do not owe any money."

"I will tell you for the fourth time…"

You can make all the laws demanding equal protection you want, but the Blacks and Mexicans always get the short end of the stick.

My case was next on the docket, and I hoped the judge didn't remember me. When he called my case, he greeted me by name, but my name was on the court file so it could be he was just easing the tension.

One thing was certain, if he remembered me, Judge Frost would never side with me. From my last appearance in front him, it was clear he didn't like me. It's not enough to ardently and correctly present the facts and the law of the case. You have to give the judge a reason to side with you. He has to like you, or your client. Without that reason, he could hang his hat on the smallest, most insignificant allegation by my opponent and, however irrational or unfair, despite the facts or the law, he would concoct a way to rule against me. Whatever reasonable or plausible legal or factual argument I made, he would rule the opposite.

My new client was driving home from work and having trouble seeing with an unusual onslaught of fog, when he decided to pull over and park in a field. He was cold, so he opened a bottle of tequila he was fortunate to have carried with him from the liquor store. He quickly got drunk, fell asleep in his car — the heater on so he wouldn't freeze. The police stumbled across the car, its engine still running, did a roadside sobriety test (which he failed) and arrested him. My client didn't understand why he got charged when he wasn't even driving.

No accident. No harm. No big deal. He thought he was being responsible. In fact, he was grateful for being woken up. Thank God the officer came along. What if — while he was sleeping — he had been mugged? He even tried to give the arresting officer a hug.

"If you fall asleep drunk in the backseat of a parked car with the ignition on so the heater is running, you are driving intoxicated," I explained, as we prepared for court, referencing precedent. "Possession of the key means possession and control of the car."

"I wasn't driving."

"Legally, you were driving. You were driving intoxicated — while you were sleeping."

"But that's ridiculous," my client said.

"That's the law."

I liked my new client, and he had been in trouble for drunk driving before, which is why he didn't drink and drive. He called me 'Barrister' and 'Esquire' as a sign of respect, sometimes with a fake British accent.

In examining and discussing the case, he had no defense. The police had probable cause to approach him in his vehicle which was trespassing on a field. The prosecutor had to prove he was driving with a blood level above the legal limit within two hours, and the blood test was performed within an hour of when he was taken into custody.

It wasn't the loss of his driver's license that disturbed him. Or the increase in his insurance. But the insult of probation, of performing community service, submitting to UAs, counseling, and completing alcohol and substance abuse classes.

When Judge Frost sentenced my client to the classes I had to object.

"Why do you object?" the judge boomed.

Like most lawyers, I spouted out several objections in a row, hoping to successfully hit one.

"My client knows better than to drink and drive as proven by the facts of this case," I explained. "In this case, Judge, my client pulled over and parked because of inclement weather. This is a mitigating factor. He did not physically drink and drive, and alcohol classes about drinking and driving are unproductive and a waste of time. He's got an excellent driving record, and he knows better than to drink and drive. No one was harmed; it was an unfortunate misunderstanding. He's a good driver. He can drink all he wants if he doesn't drive."

My client, inappropriately disheveled, coincidentally smelling like alcohol, nodded, approvingly.

"We can't have a population of drunks walking around," Judge Frost said.

"Technically, Judge," I said, "we can. We *can* have a population of drunks walking around; they just can't drive drunk, that's all."

"Don't test me, Counselor. His blood alcohol was three times the legal limit. For his own good, he's going into rehab."

He slammed down his gavel.

24

Some prospective clients revolted against my business model, and, after my initial free consultation, retained a different attorney. I had one case where my client was nine months pregnant, and on bed rest in her home; her husband told her he was leaving her for another woman, so she hit him with a chair, breaking the chair into pieces and knocking him down. He had her arrested for domestic violence and got a restraining order against her.

I went down to the courthouse on a Saturday, bailed her out of jail, and negotiated a truce between the couple so the husband could be present at the birth of their child. A few days after the birth, she fired me and hired another attorney to file her divorce, a younger one with less experience, because he had a high-end office with a good address.

Clients like this seriously thought if they paid more at a larger firm it guaranteed a better result. Like the lawyers on television, with the marble conference rooms and free cappuccinos. Lawyers who gave themselves titles.

The philosophy of the law firm is that even the simplest tasks can be billing opportunities and that is why often you see three or four attorneys on one case. They are like termites, or better still, carpenter ants, charging fees, devouring, nibbling away at your pocket book, like cedar siding.

At a larger firm, the case would be assigned a younger, less experienced lawyer, a trainee, really, called an associate. The associate runs up fees conducting meetings, discussing the case with the junior partner. The junior partner runs up fees conducting meetings, discussing the case with the senior partner. The three of them run up fees conducting meetings, discussing the case over lunch. The paralegal, who also charges, keeps track of all the meetings and the discussions and the fees and provides a careful and precise accounting of every conversation, email, Xerox, phone message, fax, and postage stamp that could possibly relate to the case. A fortune just for looking up stuff in books. No wonder people hated lawyers.

The hardest part about being a lawyer is not mastering the rules of evidence. It's not navigating the intricacies and complications of conducting a trial. Not anticipating the strategies of opposing counsel or dealing with blistering, over-reaching, arrogant, unreasonable attorneys. Not crafting the closing argument. It's not picking a jury, correctly predicting the passions and empathies of total strangers.

The hardest part of the law practice is getting paid. The poor can't pay; the middle class doesn't pay; and the rich won't pay.

I tried to help a prominent physician in a dispute with his bank over the refinance of his mortgage. He hired me to negotiate with the mortgage company. He was behind in his mortgage, which should have been my first clue: if he's not paying his mortgage, he's not going to pay me. And after numerous phone calls and letters and consultations with my client, he didn't pay me, and I dropped him. I called this the Deadbeat Doctor case.

Some clients think because I charge by the hour, they can just pay for one hour. Once I give them the rate, if the court appearance lasts only an hour, they think that will be their total cost.

It doesn't work that way. I am either all in or all out in a case. I have to charge to review the facts, do legal research, investigate the facts, and respond to the other side's motions; two hours of preparation for every hour in court.

Civil attorneys like to run up their fees. Try to bankrupt the other side by making them defend against exaggerated, inflammatory misstatements. Each side tells his own version of the story.

If you have good facts, you stick to your story, pare it down to the simplest story possible; if your facts are bad, you discredit the story or distract the judge or the jury from it with over-reaching dead-end arguments.

Contingency cases where you work on a percentage? No way. Not for me. Only if the insurance company is going to pay.

And the best one yet, a free lawyer? Where do people get this notion?

On television, when a suspect is read his rights, the police inform him that if cannot afford a lawyer, one will be appointed for him. But they don't really mean it. Only the truly destitute qualify; even then the DA has to be seeking jail time.

Here's a problem for all lawyers, I call it the 'screw the lawyer rule.' It's really two rules, but that's not the point. First, if the client requests you order a transcript or a deposition or you request mediation for the client, and the client refuses to pay after the fact, you are on the hook. You, the lawyer, pay. That's the Rule.

Second, the client can totally and utterly fail in his financial obligations to you as his lawyer, and you might have to work for him for free. Go figure, the client can drop you at any time — regardless of your agreement with the client — but you can't drop the client without the court's permission. Unless you are lucky and the client fires you. You can be fired by the client, but you can't quit. That's how it is.

If a client ever wants to mess with a lawyer under the Screw the Lawyer Rule, he simply doesn't pay. Under Rule 121, if you want to withdraw from a case, you have to file a motion to withdraw, which the court has to approve. It's the only job with conditions where you are forced to work for free. If you don't withdraw with at least several months notice before trial, the court won't let you off the case. Even with several months notice, the judge might refuse to let you off the case. Whether you are paid or not paid, the judge is more concerned with managing his docket. The client will still owe you, of course, but the day of the hearing you will still work for the client. And you can't do a lousy job just because you aren't paid.

While you can't withdraw from a case without permission, you can enter a case at any time. You are not on a case until you file a pleading or a document called an Entry of Appearance.

One of my strategies is to prepare fully for trial but wait until the day of the trial to enter. Why? Because the over-confident opposing counsel usually won't prepare as well — if he prepares at all — if he believes a person doesn't have counsel. And once you appear, opposing counsel can't move for a continuance just because he might have prepared differently. The judge will want to proceed with the hearing.

When I first started out in my law practice, I tried to keep my fees reasonable. People would line up, I thought, if the fees were affordable.

The lawyer for the middle class. Like I promised in my admission essay.

I remember a case—a dispute with a Homeowners Association. After being hired at the last minute by a disgruntled homeowner and working on the case all night, preparing for trial, I asked the client for one/tenth of what another lawyer would charge.

"For that kind of money," the defendant said. "I'd hire a real lawyer."

After that, I upped my fees. The practice of law should be a breeze. I could charge for every time I sneezed.

25

I met with a new real estate buyer, Bryan Reading. A referral from a past client. That is how most real estate deals come about. Bryan was a single guy. The worst kind of buyer. Totally unmotivated. Content to live in a tent. The best buyers were families with a reason to move. An expiring lease. Expecting twins. A job relocation. Like my Mayflower buyers. The real estate transaction waylaid at the closing table by Attorney Donald Dennis Trickey.

With the personal pressure caused by the court's order, showing houses to prospective buyers like Bryan was fun. It was a distraction. I became a lawyer because I was bored with real estate. Now I was disenchanted with the law practice, I wanted to sell real estate again. I never got tired of it. More fun even than being a mailman. It was even easier with a smart phone.

Selling real estate in many ways is easier than the practice of law; in some ways, it is harder. In the field of law, absent an emergency hearing, you can pace your caseload and take your time. For the most part, if you come up on a deadline, you can simply ask for an extension.

In the real estate business, you have to be available when the buyer is available. Nights. Holidays. Weekends. I have shown houses on Thanksgiving Day and Christmas Eve, in blizzards, once in a tornado out East along the Interstate.

I don't know how I managed to sell homes without my smart phone. Without a flashlight app. Or a calculator app. Or a real estate app. Or a GPS app. The city, with its confusing courts and cul-de-sacs, and names from eradicated Indian tribes, was developed over periods of booms and busts. Without GPS, you could waste half an hour trying to find and show one single home. I also missed the spontaneity of getting lost and finding a charming new neighborhood or an ethnic restaurant. Technology moves so fast. Every time you gain something, you lose something.

Some real estate brokers would show a buyer like Bryan only five houses and immediately ask for an earnest money deposit to make an offer. Not me. I showed Bryan dozens of homes. It was important to me that the buyer see the houses, good or bad. He needed to see the market.

Bryan was a tax examiner from the IRS. An accountant with a badge. He was almost forty. He had a good government job with health insurance, paid vacations, and a pension. Just think: a job attending meetings. A job from which it is almost impossible to be fired.

Like a prosecutor, he was convinced that everyone was cheating the IRS, and they are, of course. He audited people who exaggerated their family size—claiming tax credits for an additional non-existent child or two. A completely understandable error in math. He also audited bank robbers. Go figure, if you are caught robbing a bank—even after the stolen money is recovered—you still pay income taxes, including the FICA. Given my tax circumstances, I was surprised he selected me as his broker.

I compiled a list of cases where I believed the opposing parties had been cheating on their taxes and gave it to Bryan. Ex-husbands from cases who had not filed taxes in years or who rented rooms out to room-mates and never reported the income. Go figure, he wasn't interested unless they owed taxes of at least fifty grand.

Bryan was looking for a starter home he could later turn into a rental. He was willing to do cosmetic fix-up on the home so long as the price was low enough. We talked of price per square foot, vacancy rates, and cash flow. He made an initial list of what his ideal house would consist of: area, price, size, age, style, lot size. Schools—which didn't matter to him, but did for resale. Proximity to work. And so on.

He only needed a roof over his head, working toilet, plumbing and electric, a wet bar and space for a pool table and a big flat screen TV; he wanted to be close to the foothills of the Rockies so he could go skiing on the weekends in the winter and dirt-bike racing in the summer. He was looking for a deal.

As an IRS agent, he was assigned a government car. He was required to keep precise records of his gas mileage and usage, not allowed to use his work cell phone or government car for personal use. I missed the Land Rover, and when I missed the Land Rover, I missed Amalia. I was forced to show Bryan houses in my (fucking) Festiva.

Looking at houses, however, we saw how people really lived. What books and magazines they read. Their music collection. Their taste in decorating and clothes. During the showings I looked for clues as to what each homeowner's motivation was for selling. I rummaged through people's mail, looking for relocation, foreclosure, or bankruptcy papers. If the house was owned by a couple, and there was no men's clothing in the closet, or if the refrigerator was bare except for some beer and some Cheese Whiz, it was a divorce. If the canned goods in the pantry were lined up alphabetically, I would mix them up a bit to make a point. A vintage pinball machine in the den, we naturally had to give it a whirl. We were not yet looking for a specific neighborhood but the 'idea of a neighborhood.' Not looking for a specific house but the 'idea of a house.' Once I understood what he wanted, I would find it.

26

In one of our discussions at the bar, Kendall asked me which was a better profession: selling real estate or practicing law. You decide...

As a broker, you put a sign in the yard, or you show houses to your friends, draft the offer over drinks and dinner, then collect an incredibly large sum of money at closing. If it doesn't close, you move on to the next deal.

As a lawyer, you gather and develop evidence, interview witnesses, conduct legal research and discovery, draft and defend motions, prep witnesses, argue over jury instructions, prepare an opening and a closing. You can be right and lose; you can be wrong and win. It is rare you win everything. Even if you win, all you get is a judgment—a piece of paper. The loser files an appeal or goes bankrupt and you get nothing.

As a real estate broker, if a deal doesn't close, you simply don't receive a commission. You find another client or work with the same buyer or seller on another deal. As a lawyer, not only do you sometimes need to force the clients to pay you, if you lose, there's Rule 11.

Under this rule, if you lose any civil case, or the court finds you escalated the case, you end up fighting with the court as to whether the suit was justified. If it wasn't, or you get a judge like Judge Solomon, you could be on the hook for the winning side's attorney fees. *Personally.* Which the winning side inflates to thousands and thousands of dollars. It's the only job I know where you may not only have to work for free if the judge doesn't grant your withdrawal motion, you can face financial ruin simply for doing your job.

The rules do have a sense of humor. Once you win a judgment, you can subpoena a debtor to appear for a deposition in court, confiscate the cash from his wallet, seize his watch and wedding ring, and ask him personal questions about his finances. This is your chance to really, really wholeheartedly fuck with him. Even The Supreme Court straight-faced calls it a deposition pursuant to Rule 69.

To become a real estate broker takes about a month of classes followed by a two-hour exam that everyone passes. The total cost is around twelve hundred dollars.

A lawyer needs an undergraduate degree and a law degree. That's eight years of college. The bar exam is two days long. The law degree alone costs around a hundred grand. You do learn a little bit of Latin.

27

A woman called me at The Overtime, distressed that her daughter was in jail for stealing a toothbrush from a grocery store. It was an unfortunate misunderstanding. The toothbrush had accidentally slipped into her pocket at the checkout line.

The woman couldn't afford to pay me, but she begged me, so I went down to the Algonquin County Court for her daughter's arraignment. I checked in with the orange-haired clerk and sat in the front of the courtroom, waiting for the prosecutor. All I knew about the case was that my client had been incarcerated for eight weeks because her mother couldn't make the two hundred and fifty dollars bail.

A prosecutor is like a lieutenant in the Army, bucking for captain. Enthusiastic to put people in jail. Usually cold, ambitious, and unforgiving. To properly defend my client, I needed to look up the actual charges and review the mens rea requirement, which means mental state in Latin. This was another useful tidbit from law school. And I needed to request discovery, which is a fancy word for saying request to review the evidence.

In my favor, the prosecution has to prove every element of the crime beyond a reasonable doubt, including the intent element;

that's a high standard. If it's an accident and the prosecutor can't prove the required level of intent, he can't prove the crime, and the case is dismissed or the client in acquitted.

Prosecutors are full of tricks, some of which I should mention. One trick is to inflate the charges, making the cost and risk of trial so great you are coerced to take a deal. Another is to deny discovery. They will give you their file all right, after they have deleted any information—911 tapes, police officer notes—that hurts their case.

The defense's job is to make their jobs harder. The trick is to be a prick but not too much of a prick. The way to mess with a prosecutor is to request a jury trial and a speedy trial, which forces the prosecutor to go to trial within a limited time period. You need to make him prove his case. Every element of the crime by a reasonable doubt. You file motions, request endless discovery, make him earn his conviction.

Do you know how many cases a prosecutor has? Neither does he. When I went to court on the "Toothbrush case," the courtroom was clogged with a long line of defendants like it was Black Friday at Walmart. The DA can't possibly take them all to trial. And because he works for the government, he only works nine to five! God forbid the prosecutor should actually have to work on a case.

This prosecutor was a new lawyer, just out of law school, not even making enough money to pay the bare minimum interest on his student loans. He introduced himself as Assistant District Attorney Freeman. A man with a title.

I met with him in the back of the courtroom. I smiled when I saw the courtroom was filled with defendants and that there were stacks of court files on the table. I smiled some more at the idea of a man named Freeman with a job of putting people in jail. Was I the only one? Surely people teased him about this.

"Prosecuting my client over a toothbrush?" I asked, as he handed me the case file for my review. "Don't you have actual crimes to worry about?"

A prosecutor is cute at this age, like a lion cub. Or a baby alligator. You want to play with him a little before you club him to death in court.

"I guess we can agree to disagree," the prosecutor said. "It's a serious crime. I know it sounds petty, but the grocery store chain is fed up with shoplifters. They have a zero tolerance policy. Besides, have you seen your client's extensive criminal record?"

He pulled out a printout of my client's criminal past. Impressive for her young age: Shoplifting. Disturbing the peace. Trespassing. Driving with a suspended license (twice). Quite coincidentally, three counts of ducking into movies without paying. He had made his point, but I needed to make mine.

"Prosecuting my client over a toothbrush?" I asked again. I couldn't help but laugh out loud.

Although attorneys are arrogant, they are also thin-skinned, fragile. Most have severe personality disorders. I'm not sure if being a lawyer made them that way or of that's why they are lawyers. Sometimes it is the laugh that gets to them. That makes them re-think what they are doing.

The toothbrush slipping into her pocket shows intent. The case was hard, it could go either way. Some fights are not worth fighting. Sometimes it's better to take the deal. The maximum penalty was only thirty days. She had already done sixty.

Time served. Justice unplugged.

28

Between appointments, I had more conversations with Kendall about Henry Louis, sometimes about Amalia, or I talked to Cora, the waitress at The Overtime. Kendall and his hunting buddies had long discussions about their hunting adventures and about the sacred right to bear arms as set forth in the Second Amendment to the US Constitution. "A well-regulated militia, being necessary to the security of a free state, the right of the people to keep and bear arms, shall not be infringed."

The right to form a militia, if need be, should Kendall become even more discontented with the government than he was already. The right to slaughter deer and elk with a semi-automatic submachine gun.

Kendall's passion was multiplied in direct proportion to the number of empty beers lined up in front of him on the bar. After a few beers, he was ready to use a Bazooka.

Considering all of Kendall's problems with his divorce, I didn't want to upset him about the infringement of his civil rights. Sure, he had the Second Amendment, which no one should take away, but there were other constitutional rights that deserved his passion and attention.

"The right to bear arms is a significant right," I opined. "Whatever did the pioneers do without AK-47s? God forbid, if you are hunting for food like the pioneers, you'll likely starve without one."

He never heard me. He kept ranting about his right to bear arms, this; his right to bear arms, that. You would think The Overtime was under siege.

"Kendall," I said, finally. "Why do you suddenly care so much about your Second Amendment constitutional rights? You've already lost your First Amendment right to freedom of speech and assembly, your Sixth Amendment right to counsel, and your Fifth Amendment Right to Due Process. It's called the Patriot Act.

"And your Fourth Amendment right to privacy against illegal search and seizure," I went on. "You lost that one, too. Go ask the government if Google is listening for them! Are you listening, Google? Not once did you complain about losing these rights. You did not say a word. You just sat back and watched them slip away."

After that, he never mentioned his Second Amendment constitutional rights again, either.

The conversations with Cora, on the other hand, were less intense, more enjoyable. Almost like flirting. She stood by her waitress station, looking at a book that she pulled from her backpack. When I finished my Rueben, and she took my plate, I talked to her.

"How do you like working at The Overtime?" I inquired.

"How do you think?" she complained, crumpling up her face to reveal her dimples. "Duh! It's a shitty waitress job."

"I guess it was a ridiculous question," I said.

"No, you're fine," she said. "As far as shitty waitress jobs go, I like working for Kendall. And the hours are flexible. I like Kendall. I liked his X, too. I used to work with her here when she was a waitress. We were buds. I can't believe what the two of them have done to Little Hank."

She gave Kendall's X, formerly merely an object of disdain, a name.

I made a comment about a song, "Layla," that was playing at the restaurant. I listened to the roaring guitar licks over the sound system. She squinted her little eyes, and showed off her band T-shirt beneath her red apron from a band I never heard of. I must admit, I was mostly looking at her boobs.

"Dad rock," she said.

"What's that?"

"This song. 'Layla.' It's dad rock. Music my dad listens to."

I noticed several law books on the edge of waitress station. She explained she was taking a basic course in business law at a community college. It turned out Cora was returning to school to get an undergraduate degree, then a master's in history; after that, law school.

She had her reasons. She had had a brief marriage and a nasty divorce, and she lost custody of her daughter to her ex-husband. She was limited to supervised parenting time.

"Judge Frost or Judge Solomon?" I asked.

"Actually both. How did you know?"

"I've had cases before both of them. Why do the master's?"

"History always interested me," she explained. "I'll look really good on paper. I'll be able to get a good job. And get my daughter back."

I thought about this for a moment. A judge won't know or care about her graduate history degree. A judge doesn't base his rulings on what law firm you work for or how you look on paper. A judge won't know or care on how nice your office is or if it is located downtown or in the basement apartment. He doesn't say you are from a better firm so you win.

"It's a good plan," I said. "But I'd skip the master's. Just graduate under-grad and get the law degree and go to court and get your daughter back."

As I lectured her, she smiled, looking at me with her big brown eyes.

29

Another day, I met a new prospective client at The Overtime who wanted to retain me to file for a divorce. I was talking to Cora who was busy with the lunch crowd when the prospect arrived thirty minutes early. I hate clients who are too punctual; it shows they are controlling. It's rude. Here am I busy working on another case, and a prospective client comes in, and I feel the pressure of her waiting for me across The Overtime. But I immediately forgave her as soon as I saw her.

I must say, if ever I was tempted to start a sexual relationship with a client, this would be the one. After the case was over, of course. I could easily see myself ridding my new client of her soon-to-be ex-husband, and, maybe months later, after enough time had passed... my thoughts wandered off for a second and then wandered back to the case. Although she was probably in her late thirties, she had aged well; beautiful lips, a sensual curved neck. She had a rich, Southern drawl.

As I introduced myself, she let out this warm vibe. I made her fill out the questionnaire while she waited. Questions about the date and history of the marriage, names and addresses, the number of children, any instances of domestic violence. All based on statutes and precedent that I would need to file her case.

I noticed by her questionnaire she lived in a prestigious area of overpriced bungalows and Tudors that surrounded a big park near downtown. The park had a lake and a boathouse. Amalia and I used to go down there some afternoons in the summers for picnics and free concerts. I think part of my attraction to her, however, subconsciously, she reminded me of Amalia.

I never really thought that I had a type. I guess I do. I never liked the competitive career women, and just as important, they never liked me.

This woman was warm and kind. She was of Spanish or Mexican origin, but unlike Amalia, she had been totally Americanized. She spoke perfect English, ate bland food at The Overtime, though she dressed flamboyantly. She worked as a branch manager in a bank. She complained about the inflated prices of real estate and the ridiculous number of Starbucks. On street corners. In grocery stores. In strip malls. Being a banker, I guess she did the math, and $6 a cup is a lot for a cup of coffee.

She confided her husband had not touched her in a year. Unbelievable! I wanted to leap out of my chair and kiss her. I hadn't touched Amalia in over a year, either.

The first thing I did, I asked her if she and her husband could reconcile. There's a ninety-one day waiting period for a divorce, to give the couple time to cool off, maybe go to counseling.

If the parties went through a divorce, I could make thousands of dollars. If the couple can't get along in the divorce, and both get lawyers, a couple can blow through their life savings. If the parties reconcile, the divorce is either dismissed or never filed, and I earn, well, nothing. Amalia called this "chewing my paw."

I thought again about my divorce. Some of the arguments with

Amalia were just silly.

One time, we fought over a banana. I had left a banana on the kitchen counter the night before court to pack with my exhibit books. I usually brought a snack to help me through a whole day trial. Some judges allowed you to bring food into the courtroom to eat on the breaks; others didn't. Without even telling me, she ate the last banana.

I have to admit, at the time, I was furious.

Another time, she packed me a lunch, put it in my briefcase, and took out my notebook with all my notes for a hearing. I appeared in court, totally unprepared. Sabotaged by Amalia. Lucky for me the case was continued. We went round and round as to who was at fault on this one.

My arguments with Amalia were passionate; never violent. They almost always ended in laughter. For a few years, we had a dog, Knuckles, though the dog eventually died. One day we took him to the vet. She wrote the dog's name down on a form at the vet's office: 'Nuckles'. I informed her the word began with a silent K. The word didn't register with her, and she had a hard time believing me. I can still hear her making the K sound, trying to pronounce it, trying to make sense of the word.

The English language mystified her. The next time she wrote out a grocery list, along with the milk and some more bananas, she asked me to pick up a package of 'knoodles'.

I may not be the best one to give a guy marital advice, but still, here goes: Sleep with your wife from time to time. Be nice to her. Otherwise, keep your penis in your pants. These, along with financial difficulties, are the main causes of a divorce.

I explained the essence of a dissolution of marriage, showing off my knowledge with citations of statutes and case law. The first step after a divorce is filed — the parties exchange financial statements and supply the supporting documentation. I call this making the pie. Once you make the pie, you divide the pie, calculating how to fairly distribute the personal property, the assets and debts between the parties. Every asset is taken into account. From the smallest savings bond to the parties' coin collection, each coin valued and divided coin by coin. The court will even divide the porn.

A divorce works like this: most lawyers review the financial documents, and based on the factors in the statute, calculate what their client is reasonably entitled to. Then they double it. So they will stay employed.

The most accurate definition of a divorce I copied from a well-respected, influential, and prestigious legal journal.

"A divorce is a domestic legal proceeding which takes a highly dysfunctional family, and legally divides it into two highly dysfunctional families." That was the best definition I ever heard.

I gave her advice about the fundamentals of a divorce. There were statutes about temporary orders, how child support was calculated, parenting time was determined, alimony figured, property, pensions, and debts divided. Hopefully, there's not much to fight about. If there are no children, thank God. That's where people fight the most. They also fight about money, until they see how much money they will have to spend to fight about the money. First, a couple doesn't need to agree to get a divorce. That hardly makes sense. If a couple cannot agree on who will pay the sewer bill, they cannot agree on the divorce. Second, if one party says the marriage is broken, it's broken. End of story. Agreements of the parties or other court orders are enforced through contempt proceedings, which is an allegation of a deliberate violation of a court order under Rule 107. There are two

121

types of contempt: punitive and remedial.

Remedial contempt is when the judge is mad enough at a party for violating a court order, he or she can put you in jail until you comply. Punitive contempt is when a judge is real mad, he or she can simply put you in jail. (Amazing, though, how a deadbeat dad who owes back child support, has no money, no job, no savings, and no prospects—through some miracle of math or accounting is able to purge a remedial contempt by coughing up ten thousand dollars after spending only one night in jail.)

The smartest thing any divorcing couple can do is sit down and work out a compromise. Settle some of the divorce or all of it ahead of getting the lawyers involved. Write it on a napkin and sign it. It doesn't matter what form it is in.

A guy usually knows he has to share the assets of the marriage with his wife, especially if the wife is a housewife. A woman thinks differently. She doesn't like to share. All of the assets are hers; all of the debts are his. That was the story of my divorce.

I gave my prospective client some good advice: "Empty all the bank accounts," I suggested. "If you don't, your husband certainly will. Once he finds out you are thinking about filing the divorce."

This was sound legal reasoning. Before a divorce is filed, there are no court orders in place to protect the assets so the court can divide them fairly. One parent can run off with the children. Or abscond with all the assets and gamble them away in Las Vegas. Once the divorce is filed or if the money disappears in contemplation of the divorce, you will have to fully account for yourself and your finances.

30

A few days later, my beautiful new divorce client came up with a small retainer. It was likely the only money I would ever see from this case. She had, after all, followed my advice, and cashed in the couple's savings. That led to all kinds of problems, and, after interviewing her again, it appeared she might be in physical danger from her husband.

The first step in acquiring a Temporary Restraining Order is to file a complaint in court and then ask for an emergency hearing. I met my client at the Algonquin County courthouse for a hearing with the duty judge. An ex parte proceeding. More Latin. That means the husband wasn't notified.

My client sat in a chair in the clerk's office with a clipboard and a pen and wrote short, simple, and convincing sentences about why she was afraid of her husband. She had to swear to it under oath and penalty of perjury in front of the court clerk. The clerk's office was filled with women who were crying, hiding their bruises behind makeup and sunglasses. Who knows what these women weren't telling? Women are secretive about their abusers, or they think abuse is normal.

I have handled so many restraining orders I lost count. I

litigated a divorce where a husband tried to purchase their child from his ex-wife for one thousand dollars; another who withheld the child from his mother for a month because the wife was awarded the BMW. I took on a custody dispute where the boyfriend had broken his vow of celibacy outside of marriage by fathering his child. He impaled his penis because God instructed him to through the radio. ('And if thy right eye offend thee, pluck it out.')

I took a case where the husband wanted rent for the length of the marriage. Rent! Because he had paid the mortgage throughout the marriage. Imagine if I demanded rent from Amalia for all the years I paid the bills.

Another case where the husband admitted he tried to strangle his wife. This case was weird because he testified against himself and he didn't even apologize. He explained it in court to the judge. He thought it was totally justified. Months and months of legal work to free her from this jerk.

"It wasn't my fault," he explained. "I didn't mean to strangle her, but she drove me to it; she wouldn't shut up." And he was surprised when the judge threw the book at him.

That case was an eye-opener. After the divorce, and after the temporary restraining order was dropped, and the second temporary restraining order was granted and also dropped, and even after the counseling, she decided to go back to her ex-husband. Almost immediately, they had another row, he held her with a knife to her throat, and SWAT was called. He did sixty days in jail. After his release — and after all my work to get her extricated from this guy, she took him back a third time. I dropped the case but the consequences were predictable.

When I got my law license, the first time I was sucked into a situation of depravity and senseless violence, I was stunned; I felt shocked, guilty, helpless, the unfairness of it. I wanted to undo it. I wanted to make it right.

By now I have learned that the situation is by no means unique. Over the years, I have read hundreds of thousands of hateful texts and emails, seen the photos of the bruises and broken doors, the smashed trash cans and damaged cell phones, read the diagnosis of broken ribs and punctured lungs in hospital and police reports, heard numerous tales of child abuse and abandonment, domestic abuse, jealousy, rape and sodomy at knifepoint by angry Xs.

When my new client was finished with her complaint for her hearing, I reviewed it and noticed it was filled with typos and misspellings. I am always amazed at the poor spelling and grammar of perfectly successful and educated people like my client. When she titled her statement, sworn before the court clerk as a notary, as a 'Motorized' affidavit, I did not correct the document in any way. This document should come from the client, written as is, and besides, her poor spelling gave her more credibility than if her lawyer wrote it. It made her seem more like a victim.

I took the form to the clerk, and the clerk arranged an immediate hearing. As we waited in the back of the courtroom, I explained the process to her.

There would be a brief hearing in front of the judge where my client would simply have to tell her story as to why she wanted a restraining order. Then in about a week there would be another hearing with her husband present to give him a chance to explain why the temporary restraining order should be lifted. These hearings would have nothing to do with the divorce, and the property issues in the divorce would be litigated much later. No reason to be nervous, these restraining orders are usually granted.

The trick in law was in finding the magic words and applying them to the right situation. You have to say them exactly, like a spell. In this case all she had to say was that she was in imminent danger of irreparable harm. Physical. Psychological. Mental abuse. It didn't matter.

"Just tell the truth," I explained.

"What if he didn't do anything?" she whispered.

"What do you mean?"

"Well, he knows I am thinking about getting a divorce, but he's been pretty nice. He was mad I closed the bank accounts."

I had to think about this for a minute. If he didn't threaten her, why did she want a restraining order? It was clear she was distraught, and she didn't want to reconcile; she wanted him out of the house. But as a lawyer, I wasn't allowed to lie to the court. There are rules on these things. Mischaracterize, yes. Exaggerate, absolutely. Flat-out lie, no. And I wasn't allowed to put a witness on the stand if I knew she was going to lie.

A point for the book. You need to learn not to lie, but rather 'misremember' well if you are going to be a good witness. There is no god to send you to hell for misremembering in court. Neither will the court. It's not perjury just because the judge doesn't believe you. If the judge doesn't believe you, you don't go to jail, you simply lose.

I gave her some suggestions for her testimony. Fill in the blanks. She was afraid of her husband because... he was bigger than she was... her husband was a deputy sheriff. Better, really, if I didn't know.

"Just tell the truth," I repeated, crossing my fingers. A concept strongly encouraged by the presenters at the ethics seminar.

When the case was called, the bailiff—a fancy name for a clerk—swore her in as a witness. I had a female judge this time. A magistrate. Juanita Peach.

Magistrate Peach had been a paralegal for years, then went back to law school and became an advocate for children in truancy, dependency, and neglect cases. She was in solo practice for a while. She had no children of her own, so she viewed the children in her cases like her own, sometimes even resorting to making her rulings in simple language, like some kind of baby talk.

She almost always—if not always—sided with the female in divorce and custody cases. Women judges tend to be a little harder than men, tend to lord their authority. It's understandable, given the many difficulties a woman has to face to pursue her profession.

For a woman to become a judge, she has many obstacles to overcome, she has to learn to change her entire way of thinking. To "think like a lawyer." To rationally and logically sift through the details of the evidence presented and neutrally apply the law. Not to make snap judgments or emotional decisions. In other words, to become a judge, a woman has to learn to think like a man.

It was good I had Magistrate Peach for this case.

Magistrate Peach was short and plump and in her shiny black robe; she looked rather like a plum. The field of law is a field where you can be physically unattractive, if not ugly, and still thrive. There are few fields like this. Law and computer programming, perhaps the only two.

Men judges looked distinguished in their robes. Authoritative.

127

A man in a position of power. It's a turn-on. Women judges look unfeminine. Authoritative. A woman in a position of power. It's a turn-off. To me.

I have fantasized over hundreds of women in my lifetime. I have dreamt of making love to them in various scenarios. I even succeeded with a few. In several states and on several continents even. Not just real estate brokers, loan originators, and title reps. I did it with successful business women, corporate executives, and entrepreneurs. I slept with a girl with a trust fund in the dorm back in college. I never made it with a judge. And I had no interest in Magistrate Peach.

Once court was in session, I recited the need to protect my new client from her husband who—because of his violent and contentious conduct—placed my client in "imminent danger of irreparable harm."

The magic words.

Had my client's husband been physically or verbally abusive? Magistrate Peach inquired on the stand. Had she gone to a battered woman's shelter? How did he threaten her? Did she file a police report? Why was she so afraid?

"Last night at dinner," my client complained, crying, "after he learned I emptied the savings account, my husband stomped his feet on the floor and glared at me."

"You poor dear," the magistrate said. "Do you need a moment?"

The bailiff handed her a tissue.

Bingo. That's all it took. Temporary Restraining Order granted. Courts erred on the side of caution.

She now had sole possession of the family home. She could

safely and leisurely 'divide' the silver, the Hummels, the antique china. The family photographs, the jewelry. The kitchen stools. Toss out her husband's golf clubs and his tools. A leg-up in the divorce. She had about a week to ten days alone in the house before there would automatically be a full hearing as to whether the restraining order would be lifted or made permanent.

At the final hearing for the divorce, the judge will never waste the time going through every fork and spoon—the pots and pans of the case—or fight over a Hummel. And that's how you divide personal marital property in a divorce.

Justice preserved!

31

The holidays were approaching. Heavy snows and cold spells were coming and going, and the real estate market slowed. The best time for Bryan to look at houses; in the dead of winter, there are very few buyers. Most sellers pull their houses off the market, the remaining sellers are motivated. What I've always said, the best time to buy a home is Christmas Eve in a blizzard.

Bryan was in the midst of a new IRS case auditing some proud but disgruntled patriots who lived in a compound in the mountains and claimed they didn't have to pay Federal income taxes because their land—deeded personally to some ancestor by President Benjamin Harrison—was an independent, sovereign, nation. But he stayed on target.

I found him the perfect house for a single guy: a fix-me-up with a hot tub in the living room, a wet bar in the family room, and a nice, workable space for a big flat screen TV. A monthly payment lower than rent. What more could he possibly need? We looked at it six times. It was different looking at houses with a single guy as opposed to a guy with a girl or with a female buyer. With a man, it's about price and construction. With a woman, it's more about style, decorating, and finish. Leave the foundation for the home inspection.

I've found that almost everyone is a little racist. Even Bryan Reading.

"I'd like to buy this house," Bryan said, when we were talking about making an offer. "I'd like to Jew them down—no offense."

I told him although I wasn't Jewish, I *was* offended by the phrase. But not offended enough not to write up the deal.

"Not all lawyers are Jewish," I replied.

He paused for a moment, looking me over head to toe. "It's okay," he said, after a while. "I respect the Jews, I really do. But I completely understand. You don't have to be ashamed."

He deliberated over the house for several days, ran the numbers, fussed and fretted by text, phone, and email, and finally decided to come in with a low offer. I had to wonder. People used to live in caves and beehive huts, and in some places in the world they still do. Here Bryan complained because the house wasn't near his tennis club, and he didn't have a separate room for the Wii.

Now I don't mind if a buyer comes in low. The lower the better. The lower the price, the more satisfied the client, who will think of me when it's time to sell, years down the road. No one wants a real estate broker who gets them an average deal.

I had to warn him the house was priced well. Price is the key to real estate, and location, location, location. Proximity to a buyer's job and to good schools. Interest rates and unemployment rates are a factor.

And when the Broncos win, the buyers are all happy and enthusiastic; when they lose, the market drops and the buyers like to put their big house purchase on hold.

I warned him the house could sell. "Let's hope the Broncos keep losing," I said.

Then I noticed he was wearing a gaudy orange and blue hat: the team colors. He looked at me; he shrugged. Then he grinned.

Business is business. If this one deal goes through, I make eight thousand dollars in commission, I can pay some bills, perhaps survive the winter, and Bryan and I can go out for happy hour at Marlowe's or chimichangas at Illegal Pete's. If the deal fails, debt collectors will keep hounding me, and Bryan and I will look at more houses in the Festiva in the snow.

No, I don't mind if the buyer comes in low at all.

It turns out, I was only partly right. The Broncos fumbled their way out of making the playoffs, but the house sold anyway. Bryan was outbid by another offer.

"I guess it wasn't meant to be," he lamented.

"What do you mean?" I inquired. "Meant to be? You think the deal was pre-ordained to fail? Millions of people with problems on the planet, you think God cares about your home purchase? It's a real estate deal, for Chrissake."

"Everything happens for a reason. The deal wasn't meant to be, that's all."

"Yes, everything happens for a reason. In this case, the reason is, you came in too low. If you really wanted the property, you could have come in higher."

I went through a panic. The HUD house where I was crashing had so many showings, indicating that HUD had lowered the price to the level it would receive multiple offers. When suddenly the showings stopped, I looked on the internet, the home was under contract.

A few days later, I saw a van in front of my house, indicating that the home was going through a home inspection. There was a Lexus parked in front of the house, no doubt the realtor, trucks of contractors giving bids, and a blue Dodge minivan, presumably the buyer, in the driveway.

Later, when I went to the house after all this commotion, there were these little charcoal canisters in the hallway. The canisters sit in the home for two days to measure the radon. Sometimes a seller will open all the windows or even take the canisters outside to make sure the home passes. I wanted to make sure the HUD house failed. I shut all the windows tight and put the radon canisters in the darkest, dampest part of the basement. After the requisite 48 hours for radon testing, I put the canisters back where I found them before the inspector returned.

I didn't want to move; I hated change. I was finally settled in there. Frantically, I went out looking for a new house to crash. The inventory was down, and none of the repossessed houses I found compared to the one I lived in on Hickory Lane.

A good HUD house is hard to find. I didn't mean to be so picky; finding a place to live was tricky. I was an attorney, after all. I deserved someplace nice.

I looked on the internet to check the purchase status, the home was now available, and the showings started up again. The home must have failed the inspection, perhaps the radon test. HUD refuses to make repairs, and I was the beneficiary for now.

32

Over the holidays, which seemed to last forever, I spent too much time alone. Occupying myself with law appointments and conversations at The Overtime. Showing houses to Bryan. Catching up with bills and errands. Doing laundry and other depressing pastimes. Still driving obsessively by Amalia's house, the Festiva sputtering noisily every time I snuck down the street. The muffler was shot.

I reviewed my cases. There was Melanie's conflict with the homeowner's association, but nothing was needed on that case right now. The Homeowner's Association was still insisting that Melanie had failed to follow the rules by painting her house without the association's permission; even though the paint looked good, and the color was an approved color. I didn't think there was much of a case there.

Kendall's domestic disputes could always flare up, but I didn't charge him much because of our deal. And my new divorce case, I had already spent my client's small retainer on the restraining order. Hopefully, at any moment, something good would walk through the door.

Amalia worked through the holidays—a fact I confirmed once

or twice by driving by her office. On the weekends, I felt the coldness of her stare back at me as I drove by the Three Lakes house.

It was an off-year for elections. But still there was the noise and nonsense of living in a swing state. I was still inundated with junk mail, TV ads and faxes. Candidates who promised to lower taxes.

I voted against the retention of Judge Solomon. Obviously. And Judge Frost. I voted against the retention of Judge Tezak, whom I admired. I voted against Judge Kellogg, Judge Rodriguez and Judge Zook, a female judge whom I had never been in front of. I voted against all the judges. Just because.

And it did not make me feel any better.

I know Amalia missed her family this time of year. When we were married, she ran up hundreds of dollars of international phone calls talking to her favorite relatives. Cheaper to send her home.

I don't know about South America, but the holidays here were definitely better when I was married to Amalia. Her favorite holiday was Halloween. She decorated the porch with fake spiders and carved pumpkins, dressed in a black hat with thick green makeup and handed out handfuls of candy. She did not understand Thanksgiving. It wasn't her holiday. Each Christmas, Amalia decorated the Three Lakes home, got all emotional and phoned various lost family members. She had a red and green clock in the kitchen that played Christmas carols in Spanish.

This was the first year Amalia and I didn't spend Christmas together. We didn't even exchange presents, but I still went shopping. It was always hard to shop for her. If I bought something she needed—like a wok—she loved Chinese food—I did so at my own risk. This year, I thought about buying tickets to the ballet, with the hopes she would invite me. Amalia attended the Nutcracker, which played every year. You'd think tickets for that would be easy to find. There would be coupons or discount performances. Or even give them away for free.

After all, how many years in a row can you perform the same ballet? Or the stupid French Canadian clowns — the Cirque De Soleil? Both were sold out. The entire Christmas season.

Anything else I bought — a designer purse or socks (or anything branded European) — she would return it, I think, just because I bought it. Even if she loved it, she would never admit it. No matter what.

I walked through the mall, looking for her Christmas present. Gorgeous young women who would cringe if I spoke to them on an elevator were forced to smile at me. A man in a grey suit carrying a walkie-talkie followed me around. How dare I even glance at that expensive jewelry! I was definitely out of place. I waited for him to approach me. Another fan? I guess not. He simply lurked behind me, glaring. As I passed one designer shoe store, I noticed a sign in the window: 'Buy One <u>Pair</u>, Get One <u>Pair</u> free.' That change made me smile.

New Year's Eve was even a bigger holiday. I wondered who she celebrated with this year. She usually lit candles, wore red underwear for love and romance, chanted prayers, and practiced witchcraft, splashing water around the corners of the roof of the house for luck. She carried empty suitcases as a wish for travel. She ate a dozen grapes, exactly at midnight, one for luck for each month of the upcoming year.

Except the year of the millennium. That year, the news was flooded with disaster warnings about Y2K, and how on New

Year's Day, all the computers in the world would crash because they were not calibrated for the year 2000. On New Year's Eve, we stocked up on pet milk, spam, Oreos, and bottled water, and camped out in the basement of the Three Lakes house, listening to my old records. If we were going to go out, we would go out with music. The next day, I walked upstairs, the stove still worked, the sink, the refrigerator, even the internet (which was dial-up) worked fine. The TV was filled with New Year's cheer, advertisements for holiday sales, parades and football games. It was a new day, a new year, a new decade, a new century and a new millennium. And that's how the 21st century started: with a hoax.

I spent New Year's Eve with my mother who was celebrating she had taken her flu shot.

I thought about all the real estate deals that had failed that year, money that I left on the table, and cases that I won or lost and why. I sometimes thought maybe I was lucky even with all of my problems.

33

My mother liked to hear about my cases so she could brag about
me to her friends. The stories filled the air while I visited her over
the holidays. Quite the legal expert, Mom. She knew a lot about
the field of law from watching television. *Judge Jillian*, specifically.

Judge Jillian was an actual judge, who looked like a grouchy
old grandma in her black robe. Her television show featured cases
before her in a New Jersey court. The cases depicted were real, the
parties were real, and the litigants were bound by Judge Jillian's
rulings.

The Plaintiff on TV this time was a fine young woman, well-
dressed, attractive, professional, obviously gainfully employed.
She had put up with her deadbeat boyfriend with a ponytail,
posted the grand sum of $500 in bail money for his DUI arrest,
and shelled out some more money for a down payment on a car
for him, which, being in and out of jail and perpetually
unemployed, he never paid back.

After his most recent release from custody, his bond was
released but he pocketed the bail money, refusing to pay her back.
He cheated on her with the girl's best friend, the happy couple
broke up, and she kicked him out of her apartment. The woman

wanted back rent, the bail money, and car money reimbursed. The Defendant, the ex-boyfriend, had a cheesy little smile. He was again recently released from jail, was again unemployed, and appeared with yet another new girlfriend. A real poon hound. This was a guy who definitely tried the milk without buying the cow.

It was a tough case. He said, she said. It could go either way.

Now I must admit, Judge Jillian was a fine example of a judge. She was an exemplary judicial officer. A modern day Learned Hand. Like a real judge, Judge Jillian was moody, crazy, and irascible; she made her rulings on assumptions and first impressions, not on a neutral application of the facts and law. And she never cited a single precedent, statute or rule. Never.

"It's an inter vivos gift," I observed during the string of commercials. Showing off tidbits I learned in law school.

"Don't be so sure," my mom surmised. "It sounded like a loan to me."

"What are you complaining about?" Judge Jillian scolded the woman on TV. "Thank God you didn't marry this bum. Why should I side with you? He was your boyfriend, you picked him!"

The man looked at his ex; there was that smile again. God forbid, he mumbled something.

"Shut up!" Judge Jillian said. "Or I will rule against you right now. Do you think you are smarter than me? I guarantee you are not smarter than me; that is guaranteed."

Clack Clack Clack. Judge Jillian slammed her little wooden gavel on the bench a few times. It was very entertaining for my mom.

"How come you can't find a nice girl like that?" my mom

asked as the TV showed the Plaintiff being interviewed again, smiling her cute, perfect smile, victorious at the judge's ruling.

"Ha! I told you it was loan," she said. "And you, my son, the lawyer."

"But Mom —"

Judge Jillian's ruling was wrong. There was no testimony about a loan or loan repayment terms. My mom was more interested in the woman on television. Mom was always trying to fix me up with the daughters and nieces of her friends in her book club. I thought she was going to jot the woman's name down from the TV and track down her phone number for me.

"A very nice girl for you," she said, looking back at the screen.

"Mom, please," I said. "I'm doing fine. Besides, I don't need to find a girlfriend to lend me bail money."

She tilted her head toward me and looked at me over her glasses with that look.

The next case on TV, the plaintiff was a fine young woman, well-dressed, attractive, professional, who had posted $500 in bail money for her deadbeat boyfriend with a pony tail...

There was a *Judge Jillian*-athon over the holidays and my mother and I watched it all. Every episode. Maybe I should have written down that woman's name.

That's what the holidays were like. My mom was in her eighties, she had TV but only basic cable. She still owned a landline with an old answering machine. No internet, not even dial-up. She had tried the internet when it first came out. I had set her up with an email account on a pc so she could email her friends at her church.

"Too many advertisements," she complained.

"It's called spam," I explained.

"It all sounds like baloney to me."

Nothing else to do but watch but *Judge Jillian*, *Dr. Phil*, and the news. That was her routine. The news every hour, thanks to CNN, as if some new tragic dramatic event occurred every hour between the news at 5 p.m. on Channel 7 and the news at 6 p.m. on Channel 9. There was little else to talk about. I was the son who didn't procreate, the one who lost Amalia. In that conflict, my mother sided with my X.

In thinking about Amalia, I began to think that maybe she was right. It's not about me. It's not about me. That's what the marriage counselors said. (Of course it was about me.)

Right after the holidays, I dropped in on Amalia at Algonquin Title and invited her out to the movies. I looked on my phone for the new movies playing in Highlands Ranch. When did the movies get so bad? They make a bad movie and then they make a sequel. There was nothing I wanted to waste my time on. But I would have gone to make her happy. She refused my invitation anyway, but she wished me a Happy New Year.

Unfortunately, she was angry. I was really behind in her alimony. How dare I suggest squandering away the high cost of a movie ticket—a movie that I would only criticize and not even enjoy—when I owed her so much money?

My life would be so much easier once the alimony payments were terminated. The winters were hard for me. Amalia called the slow winter months 'the skinny cows,' a phrase that made sense to me. Clients don't pay—and buyers don't buy—during the holidays. No doubt she had run up her credit cards. A month later she called and asked me for the name of a carpet vendor.

34

Of this project for Judge Solomon and my license, I had written not a word. I still didn't know what I had done. Maybe my cell phone had gone off accidentally in court; maybe I had mislabeled the exhibits at a hearing. Maybe the judge confused me with someone else. Maybe the judge missed his morning cup of coffee or he had a spat with his wife. Or maybe he had hemorrhoids, that's all.

I looked in the most recent edition of a certain well-respected influential and prestigious legal journal for the summary of my disciplinary case. I'd had my touch of fame, and now I would have my notoriety. Infamy. The two are often the same. I was curious as to how the Disciplinary Committee would describe my sanctions.

Apparently, my case was so significant, it was worth writing a book about, but the case was not worth being published. It was not in the journal. In a way, this was a relief. It really was embarrassing, and no one would see it.

As I read through the law firm announcements and advertisements for shared office space, I skimmed an interview with my old traffic attorney, Traffic Jack. He had recently become famous when one of his clients was arrested for driving with a ventriloquist's mannequin to qualify to drive in the high occupancy vehicle lane during rush hour. The judge sentenced the man to stand for two hours four days in a row with his mannequin safe behind the guardrail on the edge of the HOV lane, carrying a sign that said "I am a dummy."

I had to admire Traffic Jack. He kept his ear to the ground and his eye on the ball. The best way to make money as a lawyer is to focus on one type of law, and offer your services as the best lawyer in that field. No matter how repetitive, humdrum, or boring the practice might become.

It was an interesting interview, and another example of a judge's crackpot ruling. Traffic Jack was still the go-to guy in traffic cases in Algonquin County, even after all these years.

The subject of my book project was the dignity and integrity of the legal system. That's what the judge said, word for word. It was important to follow exactly the language of the judge's order, so there is no confusion later.

After scribbling some more notes for the book, I had to admit, the subject matter seemed rather dull. A book about real estate sales would have been far more interesting. It would be so much simpler. The stories I could tell.

There were too many films and TV shows about lawyers anyway. What about the noble real estate broker, driving around in his luxury sedan, putting deals together? Who would tell his story? For example, there's the story about a man who sold his house, moved out, kept a key. For several weeks after closing, he came back unannounced to use the john. There was the story about a little old lady who owned a swing club. Another story about a broker holding a vacant open house that turned into a five day party.

As a real estate broker, I had experienced house showings where I walked in on people fucking, farming pot, collecting swastikas, building arsenals. The buyer who called me to look at houses by the airport because he needed to catch a flight to St. Louis. I once showed a cabin in a remote are in the foothills, down near Evergreen. When I entered, I announced that I was in the home, and no one answered. I heard rustling in the home, and no one answered a second time. I saw the back of its head, it was a bear. The buyer and I tore out of there, and I'm not sure who made it to the car first.

I had one buyer from Brazil who had never seen a dishwasher, a washing machine, or a central air conditioning unit. Same client, driving around with me through the neighborhoods to look at houses, looking for real estate yard signs. It was an election year, and there was a candidate running for mayor named Mary Taylor. She had her blue and white campaign signs in front of many of the houses throughout the area. Vote Mary for Mayor, the signs said. There was probably a half a dozen campaign signs on the block.

The buyer asked me to check on all these properties.

"This Mary Taylor, she sure has a lot of houses for sale," he said, pointing to a house across the street. "Check on this blue house, check on the one on the corner."

"No," I explained. "Those houses aren't for sale. They're just having an election."

The buyer looked at me confused. I'm not sure he believed me.

Then there was the house with the swimming pool in the living room. The meth house. The condo with black mold seeping down the walls. The house with a wolf chained up in the

144

backyard. Another house where the owner was a jazz aficionado; in the living room there was a wall full of photos, and among them, an old black and white photo of Louie Armstrong, his pants down, peeing.

Once I showed a house, and the listing broker called me before the showing to warn me about a beehive by the back door.

"Don't worry," he said, "there's bees there, I think they are hornets, but they won't sting or anything. I'm pretty sure they are friendly. You can go there, show the property. Watch out for the friendly bees."

The time I sold a house that had a murder-suicide: the husband shot his wife while she was in the can and then shot himself. Big news. Television crews. The new buyer sold tickets to strangers to view the bullet holes. I sold a home to a fortune-teller with a crystal ball, a Ouija Board, and a Tarot deck who fabricated his loan qualifications but could not foresee his arrest. The year I listed four small one-bedroom condos. I was convinced they would not sell. All four sold immediately — to young men so they could make porn to sell on the internet.

I listed a house of a black friend, and as I went through the home, I advised him to take the pictures of his family off the wall.

"A white person will not buy from a black person," I explained. "They think the house smells. I don't think that. That's just what people think. I've dealt with this issue before."

The man nodded his head. "Man, I've been putting up with this shit my whole life."

I had a seller who informed the buyers at closing that sometimes late at night she heard the footsteps of a man not her husband in the house. It sounded so eerie, like the house was haunted. Turned out, it was her brother-in-law who was a frequent guest in the house. Coming home from the late shift.

The stories I could tell. Not to mention the fraud. A book about being a real estate broker would have been so much better.

35

Some cases are resolved quickly; some drag on and on. Some are active, and then go dormant for a while, like a bear hibernating in winter. I received another letter from the HOA in Melanie's case. A certified letter this time. It had been so long since I had written to the HOA, I had almost forgotten about the case.

The HOA's response to my demand letter was to dig in its heels, insisting (again) that although the color of the home was an approved color, it was done without first seeking and receiving the approval from the homeowner's association board. The only way to correct this insult and grave offense to the board was to pay a fine and apply for official approval through the HOA and paint the home again.

The best piece of advice I gave Melanie: either comply with the HOA request or move. The second piece of advice: join the board of directors for the HOA. Become the president or the secretary or the head of the Architectural Control Committee. The HOA will not turn on its own.

Instead of moving (and I even would have listed her house for her), Melanie simply refused to get approval to repaint her home a second time. All she wanted was to be left alone. The house looked fine, better than most, and she was proud of it. The HOA board was simply picking on her. More than once, one of the board members of the homeowner's association slighted her, didn't even nod or acknowledge her, when she walked her dog Jewel through the neighborhood.

As promised, the HOA then sued her for painting the home without approval even though the house looked fine, and to repaint the front door.

"I'd rather pay you to defend me against the HOA then pay to repaint the home and the door," she said.

I know what Amalia would have said: "Don't waste my time — paint the door. Case closed."

The opposing counsel was named Gary Gary. That was his real name. He was a collection attorney who had a reputation for making up legal precedent to bully people. Or to serve a complaint on a debtor and never file the case with the court. This forces you to show up to court at the date and time on the summons, but you are not on the docket. You can't file an answer because no case has been filed. You can't file a counterclaim or learn what the case is about, but you drag yourself to the courthouse where the collection agent sits at a table in the back of the courtroom and pressures you to work out a deal without ever filing a single slip of paper with the court.

After a flurry of motions, and crazy, inflated accusations from the HOA against Melanie, Gary Gary deposed my client. A deposition is where opposing counsel (in this case, Gary Gary) and you sit around a table in a lawyers' conference room in front of a court reporter and ask your client questions. The questions are answered under oath, and the sworn testimony can be used for impeachment at trial. As Melanie's attorney, I can object to the questions but the person being deposed has to answer. The lawyer can basically ask any question he wants, within reason. And he can go back for years, drawing deep into a person's past. It's another way lawyers make easy money.

The deposition was scheduled for 9 A.M. at Gary Gary's office and was to go until the end of the day. After a couple hours of useless, irrelevant, harassing questions, Gary Gary asked my client if she had ever been involved in a lawsuit. And she answered No.

The question was a trap: my client had gone through a divorce, and a divorce was considered a lawsuit. Gary Gary was trying to use it to make it look like Melanie wasn't being honest.

I could see Gary Gary bringing it up again and again in court and insinuating that Melanie lied at the deposition, turning a simple misunderstanding about her divorce into a litmus test of credibility. If he could make my client seem like the neighborhood nut in front of the judge, the court might not believe how disorganized, vindictive, and unprofessional was the HOA.

I explained this to her at lunch, and that our conversation was privileged under the attorney-client privilege. Private communications between a lawyer and a client are confidential. Part lawyer, part psychiatrist. Part priest.

After lunch, she clarified her testimony. "I'd like to change my answer to your lawsuit question. I was in a lawsuit: a divorce. Back in the '90s."

"What was the reason for the divorce?" he demanded.

I objected.

"Please answer the question," he went on.

"How does that question lead to discoverable information?" I asked.

"I'm asking the questions here," Gary Gary said. "You've suddenly changed your testimony. I want to know why you changed your testimony and what you talked about with your client at lunch."

"My conversations with my client are privileged," I replied. "Attorney-client privilege."

"No, I have case law on this. Your client lied to me. She said she wasn't in a lawsuit. Now she says she was. I'm entitled to know about the divorce and to know what you talked about at lunch."

"On an HOA case?"

"Yes. What did you talk about at lunch?"

"Show me these lunch cases," I said.

Another note for the book: when lawyers quote the law, make them show you the cases or the statute they are referring to. Most of the time, the case isn't on point and they are (purposely) misreading it, even lying about it.

"I'm willing to move on," he offered. "I have case law."

"I'd still like to see these 'lunch' cases," I said. "Are the cases only for private conversations at lunch? What about dinner? I'd like to see a case that says opposing counsel gets to know what I talked about with my client at dinner."

"Forget it," he said. "I'll just ask my next question."

"No, no," I insisted. "The deposition is cancelled until you show me these lunch cases."

He picked up his book of statutes, the volume which contained the Rules of Civil Procedure, held it up as if to show it to me, and slowly but surely swatted the book at me, almost striking me in the nose.

"Remember *these*," Gary Gary said, holding the book up again. "These are the Rules regarding depositions. You should familiarize yourself with them. She'll answer my questions, or I'll call the judge."

"Go for it," I said. "Like the judge is going to believe you over me. And don't forget to bring your lunch cases."

He filed a motion to compel Melanie to answer the question, which motion was denied. He never did present the cases.

36

In advising Melanie on her case, I got mad again about my own situation with Judge Solomon. I applied the same advice I'd given her to become a member of the architectural control committee. I figured the best way to eliminate this ridiculous ruling against me—be appointed a judge. Judge Solomon and I would be colleagues then. We would be equals. We could joke about this project over a rousing game of badminton.

A district court judge in our state is appointed by the governor, as recommended by a nominating committee who narrows it down to three candidates for each vacancy. The only technical requirement is that you are a lawyer in good standing and have been a lawyer for five years. You have to reside in the district.

Once you are appointed you are subject to retention by the voters in the general election—with no opponent—every six years. But it's really an appointment for life. Judges are rarely voted out of office, and, unlike the district attorney or the governor, there are no term limits. It's the closest thing to royalty we have.

The nominating committee looks closely at each applicant, and the application process is quite extensive, sometimes even resulting in personal interviews. Only lawyers of the highest reputation for professionalism, fairness, honesty, and integrity are considered.

It is an important job—a judge—to be a neutral and fair decision-maker and to ensure due process and fairness throughout each court proceeding. To intelligently sift through the facts and correctly apply precedent in the furtherance of justice. Similar facts should have similar results and although the facts are often confusing, the reasoning, in retrospect, should be obvious. With such a high standard, you would think that very few lawyers would dare to submit an application. Go figure, whenever there is an opening, literally hundreds apply.

In my career as a lawyer, I had received excellent peer reviews by all of the appropriate organizations and boards. Except for this pesky order to write a book, I had never been in any kind of trouble. I was fair in my dealings with clients. Free from scandal, and my reputation was beyond reproach. With all my custody battles defending battered and abused women, I was practically a feminist, a woman's advocate. My trial success record was 50/50, which was respectable.

In contemplating applying to become a judge, I spent a few hours remembering all the trials in my career. Not the cases that settled or were dismissed, but the actual trials, with either a judge or a jury. My record was more like 55/45, even 60/40. I was far above average. Some lawyers claim they never lost a case. Either they didn't try too many cases or they cherry-picked their cases. And I was the Kryptonite Counselor, the Superman Slayer.

After reviewing the rules regarding the criteria for appointment to the bench, and a bit of self-reflection—in my totally unbiased opinion—I came to the conclusion that I was an exceptional candidate. Clearly, with fifteen years of experience, I was even a little over-qualified.

The salary was much less than I could make if I concentrated on my practice. It would be a great imposition on my life to show up for court every morning and stay there until the courthouse closes — eat the dull food at the courthouse cafeteria — sit all day long, day after day, year after year through hearings and trials, with litigants who are obviously either stupid or liars, and attorneys bickering like children. But if it helped me to eliminate Judge Solomon's order, I was willing to give it a try.

If the justice system was broken, with my track record, as a judge, maybe I could give it a whirl. Finally, a job where I could wear my pajamas to work — beneath my flowing black robe.

I could see myself, dressed in my robe, with my wooden gavel, presiding over my courtroom on the fourth floor of the courthouse, conducting weddings, issuing restraining orders, holding contempt proceedings, reading motions and reviewing exhibits, looking up precedent, and lecturing at ethics seminars. Being referred to as "Your Honor" by the clerks and security guards, former colleagues and competitors.

I looked forward to seeing the bright orange sky of the sunrise as I drove in to work at the courthouse, being ushered through security without question, and sitting with my fellow judges over breakfast meetings exchanging deep thoughts.

I imagined my own private chambers — large but not audaciously large — complete with cherry bookshelves — my own empire, so to speak. The learned Honorable Judge Darwyn VanWye. It would make Amalia proud and my mother beam.

With the health insurance benefits of a government job, I could finally have my cavities filled, my teeth cleaned. The people would rise when I entered the room, and the lowly lawyers in my courtroom would be required to laugh at my jokes. And if I said the weather sure has been cold, the clerk and bailiff and all the lawyers in my courtroom would nod and agree. No one would make a sound. As if—just because I said it—it was profound.

37

The main criterion for landing a judicial appointment was being a friend of the governor. If you want to be a judge, first become a prosecutor or a public defender. Most judges have given some of their career to public service. In considering my qualifications, I admit I was a little weak in this area.

Next, if you want to be a judge, routinely attend bar functions and rub elbows with other prominent attorneys. These attorneys could some day be governor or at least advise the governor. In considering my qualifications, I may have been a little weak here also. The only "bar" I went to was The Overtime.

Governors from one political party appoint lawyers as judges from their party, and governors from the other party appoint judges from the other party. I thought about this qualification also. The political parties were identical in many ways, burdened by extremists on both side; I could be a successful moderate in both parties and it would make no difference whatsoever. I wondered if there was a rule against joining both political parties.

The current governor appeared on television to be a very nice fellow. He smiled and posed for photographs for the one remaining newspaper while observing kindergartners at elementary schools. Smiling and shaking hands with the teachers and assistant principal. People liked the way he walked. I had a lot of insights into his qualifications from his numerous TV appearances. For example, I knew his favorite breakfast cereal—Cocoa Puffs—and his favorite beverage, Tang. I knew from important news broadcasts how much he paid for his haircut. He had good hair, it was well-documented. This governor's favorite color was blue, he only bought American cars. You would think a politician with such high credentials would be an exceptional governor.

Despite all of these important qualifications, he was a horrible little man. From a very wealthy family, he went off to study at an Ivy League school, with a degree in business, and made an even greater fortune on fracking for oil below homes in working class neighborhoods, as well as other questionable real estate development deals.

He ran a grassroots campaign, trying to convince farmers and factory workers that he was the agent of change, and by change he meant the elimination of government subsidies and benefits currently enjoyed by the farmers and factory workers. He tried to buy the election, constantly running negative, exaggerated ads throughout the election season.

He won his first term by an astounding margin of seven hundred votes, which he naturally interpreted this great victory as a mandate to enforce his draconian social measures. The first thing he did as governor—he went before the legislature and demanded a raise. As far as I could tell, the only possibly redemptive quality he had was that he liked Led Zeppelin. I would never vote for him.

Would I really have to hobnob with this jerk? Share a basket of fries and a bucket of wings? Or go someplace fancier. Would I be forced to have lunch with him at Strings?

After I conducted this research, I googled the judicial openings for Algonquin County. There were no vacancies. What a relief!

(Buffalo wings sure sounded appetizing, though.)

38

My next thought was to apply to be a magistrate. A magistrate is a baby judge—appointed by the chief judge. Except a magistrate doesn't need five years of experience. Can be appointed just out of law school. May not ever even have set foot in a courtroom. And there he or she is, hearing your case. Their qualifications: a magistrate is a lawyer who is a friend of the chief judge.

The title of chief judge is not as grand as it sounds. The chief judge has the extra job of being the administrator of a judicial division. He's in charge of the other judges, and the smooth running of the court system. He takes on additional administrative work, organizes the court dockets, determines what types of cases the judges hear, how often they rotate to hear different types of cases so they won't get bored, and settles disputes among his fellow judges. Most judges wouldn't want to do it.

I didn't respect magistrates as much as judges. In the lower courts, you can opt out of the magistrate and request a judge. It's called a Motion to Opt Out of Magistrate. I always recommend that.

As a litigant, if you have the choice, rather than being

randomly assigned a magistrate by the clerk, you might as well get the most qualified judicial officer you can find. As an added bonus, it might throw off some of these collection attorneys — who go to court Tuesdays and Thursdays with the same magistrate. And it's good strategy if you want to delay the case.

Unlike a judge — a magistrate never comes up for re-election. He is appointed for life, or for as long as the chief judge tolerates him. In other words, you can never get rid of one.

If I was over-qualified to be a judge, I was even more over-qualified to be appointed a magistrate. I looked up the name of the chief judge presiding in Algonquin County. You guessed it: Judge Solomon.

39

I always found it odd that a judge will push a felony case fast through the legal system, and make a rush to judgment, but a much less significant civil case can meander in the courts for years. Custody cases go on until the child turns eighteen, and only when a motion is filed or the courts make deadlines do the lawyers work on the case.

Kendall's custody disputes over Henry Louis had been dormant for a while, and just as Kendall began to relax, the situation with his X flared up again.

A divorce decree enters but the case lasts until all the alimony and child support is paid, the property is divided and the children are grown. After the divorce, it's not that one party cheated, or that the couple grew apart; the wounds are aggravated by the lawyers and the legal system. By what one party said about the other in court, or the exaggerations a lawyer wrote in filing motion after motion after motion.

Year after year.

The main issue was child support; Kendall thought he was paying too much – his X thought it was not near enough. This is always the case...

His X filed a motion, and Algonquin County District Court required mediation prior to conducting a hearing. Kendall approached me to attend the mediation. The judges would rather not waste their time on a half or full day hearing until and after you have wasted your own time on mediation. The court requires a two-hour minimum.

The best thing about mediation, I get paid to sit there and do nothing. Especially if the mediation is conducted with the parties in separate conference rooms.

Seriously. In these cases, I am like luggage. Half of the time is spent with the mediator shuttling to one side or the other with discussions, negotiations, offers, and counteroffers. I could literally write my assigned book on my laptop while waiting in the room for the mediator and Kendall would never know the difference.

There is a difference between mediation and arbitration, and clients are often confused. Mediation is a settlement negotiation similar to shuttle diplomacy. It is confidential and inadmissible. No decisions are made at mediation unless the parties agree to them in writing. Arbitration is an alternative court proceeding with a private judge who makes a final ruling. It is more relaxed than a formal court proceeding, and the rules of procedure and evidence are relaxed. A court proceeding without rules. A court proceeding of chaos.

The best definition of a mediation I found was in a well-respected, influential, and prestigious legal journal: "a mediation is a confidential settlement proceeding where a neutral third party called a mediator convinces each side that they will lose at trial."

My own definition is simpler: a mediator is (usually) a lawyer who is afraid to take his own cases to trial so he charges people a fortune to mess up other people's cases.

Kendall and I met with his X and her lawyer and a mediator at the mediator's office to discuss several ongoing disputes concerning Henry Louis. Along with the child-support dispute, there was a conflict over parenting time during the soccer season. Henry Louis had soccer practice during Dad's parenting time, but Mom refused to let the child participate in the soccer games because they were on her parenting time.

Henry Louis loved soccer. He was good at it, he was a fast runner, especially for his age. The child's therapist recommended that Henry Louis be encouraged to participate in soccer, and, after receiving the therapist's recommendations, discussing them and weighing them in Henry Louis' best interests, the X simply changed therapists. No soccer games on her time. The boy practiced all week but never got to play in the games, and the championships were coming up.

There was another issue of Kendall's vacation to Niagara Falls. Kendall took Henry Louis to see his aunt, Kendall's sister, in upstate New York. The family decided to take a side trip to Niagara Falls. Kendall and his sister, who allegedly posed as the X to pass the border inspection, crossed over to the Canadian side with Henry Louis.

Although Kendall claimed most of the trip was on the American side, not in Ontario, traveling without disclosing the itinerary was against the Permanent Orders as set out in the divorce decree—she was going to take him to court for contempt.

To go to Niagara Falls without giving the X the itinerary was bad enough; to cross into a foreign country was even worse.

He says he called her from customs to ask for permission; she says he didn't. It was a difficult case—he said, she said.

The X was besides herself with worry. She called the FBI, the NSA, the TSA, the border patrol, and the Coast Guard, accusing Kendall of kidnapping, attempting to disappear with the child into a foreign country. She was so desperate to contact him, she posted tweets on Twitter and Facebook, even notified Google.

All this fuss over a day trip and a nice lunch and a short ride under the falls in a yellow raincoat and a life preserver on the Maid of the Mist, captured on video by the aunt. We spent the rest of the afternoon with the mediator fighting over a significant medical bill in the amount of $7 for a prescription that Kendall ordered for Henry Louis without his X's consent. Kendall's X spent several hundred dollars in attorneys fees over this important issue.

In Kendall's defense, his X decided not to attend that particular doctor's appointment. He simply forgot to tell her about the new medication. She refused to pay her share. After three hours of bickering, his X walked out of the mediation. She was pursuing the contempt for the Niagara Falls incident, and taking him to court to dispute the $7.

Unconscionable. Unforgivable. Egregious.

Cases only settle if the parties want to settle them. Angry ex-wives and car dealerships — like the Dodge man — would rather go to court than settle, even if it costs thousands of dollars more.

I spoke to opposing counsel after the mediation. I asked him to drop the contempt, but he refused. Kendall's X really wanted to see Kendall go to jail.

Under the Rules of Ethics, he wasn't allowed to overtly threaten my client with jail for violating the court's order, so instead he had made snide comments: "I can't wait until the hearing"; "I need to teach your client a lesson"; "Remind your client to bring his toothbrush."

When the mediation failed, Kendall joked about elk season again.

Poor Henry Louis. Gifted or not, his future was undermined by his parents bickering. Someone has to grow up to work behind the counter of a convenience store.

40

Some cases are just plain weird. One of my real estate clients was accused of sexual assault on a child. He was an elementary school teacher; the incident occurred over recess. He allegedly asked a seven-year-old to carry his supplies out to his van, then took the child out to a field and inappropriately touched him.

He explained later that the child seemed to be ignored, and he believed he had the parents' permission.

"That's so gross," Cora said as I talked to her about the case at The Overtime. "I've got a solution—snip, snip," she went on, making a scissors-cutting motion with her hands. "How do you defend a person like that—who you know is guilty?"

Philosophical questions like that are left for the luxury of law students. A person is not guilty until the legal process says he is guilty. Just because he commits an unsavory act doesn't necessarily mean he committed an unsavory crime. Besides, that's the job. Guilty or not, it's my job to get him off. It doesn't mean I endorse what he did; it doesn't mean that I want him as his friend.

"Why does a garbage collector collect garbage?" I replied. "It's gross, but it's the job."

I referred him to a 'wee-wee' attorney. That's what they are called, specialists in defending against charges of sex crimes. You can google that. The attorney I referred him to charged him one hundred thousand dollars to get him off.

Unlike realtors, however, lawyers don't even get referral fees. A broker gets a twenty-five per cent cut off the top of the real estate sales commission for referring a client if the deal closes. Another reason to be a real estate broker.

41

Bryan showed up at an appointment to look at houses with a new girlfriend, Shauna. She was pretty enough; nice, well-maintained body, but absolutely no sense of humor. I have to admit Shauna was a little cold toward me. She didn't join in the camaraderie that Bryan and I enjoyed.

Bryan came up with the most memorable nicknames for houses. The house with the purple carpet in the family room. I said 'the Purple Rain house.' Bryan said 'Purple Haze.' Shauna said 'the Barney house.' Shauna's nicknames for houses were embarrassing; Bryan looked at me, rolled his eyes and grinned. We went with Bryan's suggestions—he was the buyer.

Shauna had her own real estate broker at Remart she kept touting; how this woman, her broker, had sold two or three lofts downtown just yesterday, how she drove a really nice Audi and had a timeshare in the mountains, how she could find a house for a buyer by only showing three houses. She bragged about her parents—her mom was a lawyer and her dad was a judge in Minnesota. Bryan was loyal to me as his broker; he rolled his eyes again. The connection between guys where there is no sexual tension is more genuine than the connection between a man and a woman. We must have made her feel like an outsider.

Their story was sweet; he had audited her past three years federal income tax returns one afternoon with Shauna and her accountant. Then, several weeks later, by coincidence, while he was visiting his mom—taking out the garbage—she jogged by. They recognized each other from the audit and started talking. After the taxes were renegotiated and settled, he called her up and asked her out.

Bryan and Shauna were in love. I know because they gave each other nicknames.

Shauna started calling Bryan 'Bri' or 'Bear.' Bryan called her 'Sweets' and 'Dumpling.' They frequently held hands and snuggled during house-hunting excursions. Once or twice, while we were viewing homes, I walked in on them, kissing in the kitchen. But she never wanted to give her opinion about the houses Bryan was considering.

"Well, it's your house, Bear," she said. "It's not like my opinion matters."

"I want your opinion, Dumpling." Kiss. Kiss.

A few weeks later, during another house-hunting excursion, Bryan announced they were getting married. An August wedding with a honeymoon in Hawaii. Although my first reaction was silence, I was happy for him. Life is better if you have someone to fight with. Someone to pretend to laugh at your jokes. Marriage is also good for the real estate business. It gives people a reason to make a move and usually imposes a deadline.

In this case, the deadline was July so they could be in the home before the wedding, maybe even have the reception in the backyard if the landscaping was good enough.

"Congratulations," I said.

While Shauna had been previously married, Bryan had always been single. He took me aside in the secondary bedroom at one of the houses; he was a little nervous, he confided. He was giving up his exciting and exotic single life of one-night stands and sports bars.

"You'll be fine," I said. "She likes you, that's all that matters. Give it a try. I wish I was still married."

"What about my 401k?" he asked.

Without a wife all these years, he had amassed a small fortune—by remaining single. His credit cards were not maxed-out. In fact, he was debt-free. He didn't owe payments on expensive furniture or season tickets to Broadway musicals; he had no children, which meant he had no bills for school supplies or school lunches, little league uniforms, braces, kids toys, piano lessons, college funds, summer camps, or family therapists.

"Not to worry," I explained. "Anything you owned before the marriage is separate property. It's not like marriage is for a long time. I can always get you a divorce. A divorce only takes ninety-one days."

I'm certain this encouraged him.

After studying their personal finances, and considering their combined incomes, they—meaning Shauna—revised their list of requirements for their house-hunting. A starter home was out. They doubled their price range. With their combined incomes, they could afford much higher payments.

Instead of looking at the homes on the west side of town by the foothills, with rolling hills and mountain views and an easy drive to the mountains and the ski slopes, we were now looking at the more affordable, cookie-cutter homes in the eastern suburbs of the city—which, because of their lack of trees, topography and character was colloquially referred to as 'Kansas.'

A fix-up property. Out. They—meaning Shauna—didn't want to do too much work. A pool table room. Out. Darn. Not a priority. A wet bar. Out. Drat. Proximity to dirt bikes trail. Out. Obviously.

They—meaning Shauna—were looking for a nice home at a reasonable price that didn't need too much work, good schools where they could start a family. A big kitchen with granite countertops and cherry cabinets with a family room off of it, and a master bath with a five-piece bath—a sink for him and a sink for her. And two walk-in closets: one for her, and a second one for... well... her.

Go figure. We looked at a house in an area called The Pines; a new neighborhood without a single tree in the neighborhood, not a good setting for the wedding. A house in The Farms with a tiny lot. The 'magnificent' view from a house in The Overlook—a busy street and The Home Depot.

We did find one attractive area. In The Vista, greenbelts by a creek were lined with cattails, pine trees, and weeping willows. For their upcoming nuptials, it was quite scenic. Scenic and charming.

While this setting was nice, it wasn't because the builder was an environmentalist or had some vision of creating a community that communed with nature. The designated open space was not preserved simply out of the largesse and generosity of the developer. The land had been a swamp.

"You can't build on wetlands," I explained, showing off more tidbits from law school. "If the builder had its way, it would have

171

built houses on stilts. The Clean Water Act, which protects the habitat of migrating geese — prohibits building there. And the type of vegetation — the cattails — determines if the land is protected."

Bryan and Shauna nodded politely as if this was even remotely interesting.

"And speaking of water," I went on. "There is a huge water shortage here. The aquifer beneath the city is shrinking, and everyone knows it. The city will someday run out of water, but the builders keep on building anyway."

Bryan and Shauna nodded again.

The main criterion: the home had to beckon to Shauna. It had to speak her language. As we looked at houses, she named the inanimate objects around her to make her feel more at home. She called her mobile phone, Moby. She referred to her laptop as Petey. Petey the computer.

I found them a house in The Summit they liked with a big yard and a gazebo for the wedding; I know they liked the home because as they were looking, they sat down in the family room and relaxed for a moment. Shauna placed the furniture. Where will Teddy the TV sit? Bryan expounded about the list, trying to place the pool table.

Shauna gave me a look; she rolled her eyes.

"Shut up, Dumpling," I instructed. "You don't get room for a pool table."

Bryan looked at me, startled.

"This is going to be her house," I pointed to Shauna. "Now that you're a couple, she gets to decide. She picks the house, you pay for the house. From my experience, that's how it works."

He looked sullen. No one had ever talked to him like that.

She beamed. Her house. She didn't choose this one, but she got to choose. I had won her over. She was my new best friend. She was now the Buyer. And she would bring him around. My job now was to find them a house that spoke to Shauna and to make sure Bryan went through with the wedding.

42

It was now approaching spring, although it still snowed sometimes. Broncos spring training camp began, and I had still not made progress on the book. It was the high season for real estate sales. The real estate market heated up because families with children wanted to change schools over the summer recess.

Amalia invited me to her annual party, her open house, and I could hardly wait. It would be a great opportunity to talk to her again and maybe resolve some of our problems.

South American parties were usually pretty wild—especially around Carnival. She invited her friends from various Latin and South American countries, conveniently lumped together in the United States as Latin or Hispanic and from her job, which involved personal politics and melodrama.

The people she did invite—which could be in the hundreds— appeared with their parents, their children, and their grandchildren, some helping with cooking, some with the decorations, others helping with the cleaning up. There were mariachi singers and line dances; the feast wouldn't even start until almost midnight and with the drinking and dancing, the party would last all night.

For me, these parties had been great, a huge income tax write-off, back when I used to pay taxes. As the guests arrived, everybody greeted and kissed everyone else on the cheek and they kissed again when they left, one of her Latin rituals. I found this unnecessary touching a little odd, and I often ducked out when these wrinkled old ladies with perfume and lipstick tried to kiss me.

Despite my notoriety as a real estate broker or a lawyer in most social circles, I was best known at these parties as 'Amalia's Gringo.' For me, I only had a few clients I thought of as friends, and given the mixed feeling my clients had about Amalia, I never invited any of them. If another American husband was there, she would make us sit together like we would automatically be friends just because we both spoke English.

Quarantined. Like sitting at the kids' table.

She would periodically come and check to make sure the food was not too spicy and that the American section of the party was taken care of. As if she was showing me off as her gringo.

Amalia hadn't had one of these parties for several years — what with the bad news about never being able to have children and the uproar over the divorce.

After Amalia reminded me about the party, I paced around the HUD house contemplating how the conversations would go. There was a reason she invited me, and I needed to develop a strategy. Maybe start out slow as if we were starting over.

She enjoyed music theater and live shows for the costumes; maybe we could go on a weekend getaway to Vegas.

After looking on the internet, there weren't any trips I could afford. Then I thought I should bring something to the party, a gift of some kind. After all, I had missed giving her a present over

Christmas.

She liked exotic fruit from her country, and I thought about getting her a bouquet of fresh fruit. I had seen these fruit arrangements in a boutique in the mall. Papayas and mangos and slices of pineapple on a stick to look like sunflowers.

I looked on the internet, the cost was $70 — for a few dollars worth of fruit in a basket.

At the very least, I needed to seem willing to reunite with her, but not too anxious. Nothing is worse than showing signs of desperation. What to wear? Not too casual, not too formal. When you are young, love is a mystery, an exploration.

How do you woo someone you have known for years? I can't say I had learned any new moves. Surely she knew me and all of my tricks by now.

Even the timing of my appearance was important. I needed to show up fashionably late, as if the party were an afterthought, even though, in fact, I was rarely invited to parties. I didn't want to be the sad and lonely X with nothing better to do. No matter what, I would not stay too long. I would not overstay my welcome. I would come late and leave early, after having made the right impression.

I showed up exactly an hour after the party was to begin, as I planned. Cars were lined up and down the street by the Three Lakes house. A black Lexus was parked in the driveway. The house was much tidier than when I snuck in last time.

Amalia had decorated the living room and kitchen with bright colored Carnival masks and balloons, lit a fire in the fireplace. The carpet was thick and posh and smelled new, too. An interesting teal color. Not what I would have chosen, but she didn't ask me. No doubt paid for by the divorce.

I must say, the home had many upgrades that no one else would appreciate. High-end stainless steel appliances, for one thing. A big private yard with stamped concrete in the back patio for another. When we first bought the house and we were doing the fix-up, Amalia used to joke about her real estate broker—me. If the dishwasher broke, she'd say, "I had a lousy realtor; I should have bought a house from Remart."

I noticed her familiar Argentine folk music was playing over the intercom system. Whatever depression she had suffered in our marriage and divorce, it seemed like she was getting better. I could tell already, this party was different for her.

Carnival had already passed, so this was just an open house. There were only a handful of guests, mostly Americans. No kissing or hugging going on here. There were no children or grandparents. The house was filled with people still dressed for work at their pleasant air-conditioned white collar jobs, checking their smart phones. I recognized some of them from Algonquin Title—closers, secretaries, and processors, and several of my fellow real estate brokers.

Some of the guests were my old real estate clients, mostly couples, whom I had lost contact with after the divorce. Standing in boring little clusters, drinking Lite beer. One couple I had sold a house to years ago, and as far as I know, they were still living there. They probably paid it off by now. Once people get their children enrolled in a school they stay put, they try not to move.

One of Amalia's friends—she had sold Mary Kay cosmetics and wanted to own a pink Cadillac, which the company awarded to its tops sales people. When I heard about the party, I expected she would be invited, and as I walked toward the house I carefully perused the cars parked on the street to see if she had been awarded the car. No pink Cadillac.

Years ago I had tried to sell her a home. I showed her houses in her price range for several weeks; they were never good enough. When she finally found a home, she couldn't qualify for a standard loan. I advised her to wait until her credit returned. She was convinced I wanted her to fail. She bought the home through another broker and got a B paper loan with a ridiculous escalation clause and big prepayment penalty. For several years she bragged about her house, stressing the word *house* as if her buying it was some kind of act of defiance. Finally, the loan escalated and she lost the home in foreclosure. I hadn't seen her in several years. She didn't talk about the home anymore.

I greeted them all, smiling and laughing, shaking their hands. Most I hadn't seen in a long time. Imagine my glum reaction when one of them bragged to me about how he just sold the home I sold him years ago and closed on a totally-renovated house in a very nice area called Bonnie Brae. As I recall, I had even attended his wedding. He went on and on, describing the imported Italian marble and the puck lights in the gourmet kitchen.

As a broker, you assume if you do a good job, and your client is happy, he will call you back when it is time to sell the house you sold him. You can buy him closing gifts, send him postcards and calendars, occasionally invite him out to lunch. But you can't make him call you. With this client, I failed to do any of these things. Still, this was a little upsetting. In fact, it was an act of betrayal. I did a good job for him then, I would have done a good job now. I could have used those commissions.

Amalia's friends were so dull, I was glad I didn't have any friends.

Most common questions: How is business and when was I going to do another commercial?

You always say business is great, even if you are starving. This is the impression you want to leave with this person, a potential client or source of referrals. The impression he will have in his mind should he ever decide to call you or if he runs into a mutual friend. Perhaps for years.

No one wants a real estate broker who can't close a deal or an attorney without any cases. You always say you are busy, successful, thriving. If a potential client calls to set up an appointment, you set it a week out. That is why when you call a law office the lawyer is always in a meeting and if you call a real estate office the realtor is in a closing. No one has that many closings.

"Business is great," I said, going through the small clusters of crowds, shaking hands. "Booming. I don't need a TV commercial right now. It's shaping up into an excellent year."

Standing by Amalia, Donald Douglas Trickey. The lawyer from the real estate closing with the Mayflower buyers. Although he had grown a small beard, which was touched with grey, and although it had been years, I recognized him immediately.

He followed Amalia around the kitchen while she served South American snacks as hors d'oeuvres. If she opened the fridge, he walked over there with her. If she greeted a guest, he stood at her side. Amalia introduced him to me as 'Don.'

"I'm Donald Douglas Trickey," he said. "Chief Counsel for Algonquin Title Company."

Great, I thought. I knew it was him, and I was surprised he didn't remember me; I guess I'm not as memorable as one would suppose. And now he's a lawyer with a title.

"I'm Amalia's ex," I explained, shaking his hand.

"So I've heard," he winked annoyingly.

Trickey, that mealy-mouthed little motherfucker.

Amalia had pulled her recipe book from the kitchen drawer. He now wore an apron and a chef's hat; he was cooking Argentine recipes with Amalia. They laughed and made inside jokes, and he brushed his fingers across the side of her apron as they worked.

Cooking is sensual; it's analogous to sex. He was having analogous sex with Amalia. Right in front of me.

43

I would never get the alimony terminated now. My only hope now was if she married Trickey, the alimony would terminate. That is not what I wanted. Why would she marry him?

I understand that women trade up sometimes. But Trickey wasn't even up. He was old and boring, his handshake was sweaty and slimy, and his breath was bad. How could she even be attracted to him? Yet it was happening before my eyes. It seemed so unfair. How many second chances had I gotten from DAs? Third chances from judges for my criminal clients.

Where was my second chance with Amalia?

I walked out to the garage, away from the lights and the decorations and the music, and sat on the edge of the step. I looked across the garage at the Land Rover, several trash cans, my old boxes.

First thing I did, I examined the electric garage door opener; I verified it seemed in good working order, with its cords all going to their proper places. When I pushed the button, the garage door rose about two feet; I pushed the button again, and the door dropped back down. I waited for Amalia to hear the garage door close, come and check on me. I pressed the button again. Still, no

Amalia.

I took out my phone and I googled Donald Douglas Trickey. Although I had seen his internet ads before, and even clicked on them, I needed to conduct a more thorough search. He had gone through, amicably, it appears, one divorce, and there was nothing of any concern that would disqualify him from going out with Amalia. He was simply an esteemed and well-respected real estate attorney. The Chief Counsel for Algonquin Title, representing title companies along with lenders and real estate companies. He had even won an award from the bar association for his work helping to build houses for the under-privileged and homeless.

Now I don't usually begrudge anyone his success. I've always thought awards were, for the most part, kind of silly. For a moment, I hated Donald Trickey. Trickey, the Deal-Killer, killing my new deal with Amalia.

I took my old model aircraft carrier — that I had worked on for years when we were married — lifted it up, and dumped it into the garbage can.

There was a crash. No one seemed to hear. Or care. Or at least no one came into the garage. I had installed extra insulation. The garage was pretty much soundproof... and fireproof, for that matter. Despite that, even from the garage I could hear the music, the edge of voices from the party, Trickey and Amalia laughing.

I looked through my boxes of old case files and exhibit books, rummaged through the tax returns, medical records, and police reports of former clients. Pages and pages of discovery requests and disclosures and responses and notices and motions, long ago resolved, or more precisely, never really adequately resolved.

There was the file from the divorce of a forty-year-old guy and his young Russian catalog bride. He flew out five times to Russia and courted her and paid the matchmakers — Russian Blossoms — the appropriate five thousand dollar fee for their services. When the young bride arrived, he locked her in his apartment, mentally and physically abused her, and isolated her from all contact with her family. Eventually she escaped and filed for a divorce. He threatened that if she demanded any kind of settlement, he would have her deported. The husband argued she was a foreign woman for sale who had used him for immigration purposes. What I saw was a brave, smart woman who left her family in Russia to start a life here with this guy.

If I worked at immigration, and I had to choose between my client and her ex-husband, I would choose her. Sometimes it's a shame we are stuck with our citizens. It would serve him right if *he* could be deported.

The judge bumped his case, informing him at a status conference he would continue to bump his case until the case settled. Maybe the guy was legally correct in that since the marriage failed so quickly, she could be deported, but he just looked plain mean to the judge.

Who cares? Why was I keeping these old cases?

A real estate broker is required to keep his files for four years. Hard to believe, a lawyer has no such requirement. For a lawyer, the file belongs to the client, and as long as you give the client the opportunity to retrieve it, into Amalia's trash it can go.

Goodbye Russian Blossom. Goodbye Dodge man. Goodbye to dozens of photos of an odometer and a blue Dodge minivan. Goodbye Mighty Methodist. And goodbye to whatever principle I was fighting for.

I sat for a moment and studied the space where the boxes used to be. The garage looked so empty without them, as if they had never existed. Then I realized: under the rules my client's personal documents such as tax returns needed to be burned. Or at least shredded.

You can't have people's personal information like their social security numbers laying around in the garbage for any random dumpster-diver to find.

Rules Rules Rules. I left the files in Amalia's trash.

I looked through the boxes of records, my one victory in court with Amalia. I carried my vinyl record collection out from the garage and sat on the floor in the family room by the fireplace. I had been meaning to retrieve it for some time. I walked over to the kitchen and grabbed another beer.

"Rock 'n' roll." Trickey pointed to the records, walking by me, following Amalia.

"You got it." I took a big sip of the beer.

I sat on the floor by the fireplace, listening the crackling of the wood as the flames gnawed away at the logs in the fireplace, the warmth of the fire on my cheeks. The music and the laughter and the edges of people's voices. I sat quietly by myself on the floor, crossing my legs, the records on my lap.

I didn't know what to do with myself. Amalia and Trickey were having a really good time, and Amalia didn't seem to want to talk to me. Neither did any of my old clients. I was like an old sofa, ready to be hauled out for Goodwill.

One by one, I looked through my albums, records I acquired in my youth, music I had listened to when I was dating Amalia. Even before then. Records I skimped and saved for. From high school and junior high. I pulled each record out of the jacket, examined it for scratches and cracks. Some of the records were rare. Bright, youthful record covers, trite lyrics from singer-songwriters. Most were bands long forgotten. One or two records were pretty beaten up. I tossed the jacket, and the records, one by one into the fire. With each record, I watched the flames die down, then flare up as the records melted.

"What are you doing?" Amalia asked, sitting next to me on the floor now, Trickey standing a few feet away, sort of hovering over me. I thought she would swear at me. Nothing.

"I'm trying to help you," I answered. "I'm getting rid of stuff."

"In the middle of my party?"

"Well, the records are mine from the divorce," I explained. "What do you care, anyway? You don't even like Frank Zappa. Or Jethro Tull. You don't even know what a Kink is. You don't know who The Who are."

"You!" she scolded, in that nagging voice I knew from our marriage. "Get out!"

I left the rest of the records in a pile on the floor, and walked out through the front door. I didn't mean to, but I slammed the door behind me with a 'Boom.' No one in that room would ever do business with me again. And neither would any of their friends.

As I boarded my car, I felt like everyone from the party was still watching me. I drove around the neighborhood for a while, and being drunk, got a little lost, wandering around the confusing suburban streets with their identical speed bumps and cul-de-sacs and courts and lanes and ways and greenbelts and fire hydrants and mailbox clusters.

I drove by Amalia's house once — then twice — Trickey's shiny black Lexus still parked in my driveway. I drove around for a half-hour or so, looking for young families in minivans and trying to drive them off the road. This was illegal, arguably.

As I drove back toward The Overtime, I crashed my car into the side of the wall at the entrance of Three Lakes. In my defense, it could happen to anyone. I sat there in the Festiva and fell asleep, until the police finally stumbled upon me.

44

I failed the blood test for DUI and I spent the night in stir. Kendall gave me shit for having to lend me money to post my bail.

"Eight hundred dollars!" he kept complaining.

"If I had charged you for my legal services in attending the mediation, I would have had money to spare."

"Eight hundred dollars!" he said again.

I had never been in jail before, although I had visited clients there, and it wasn't as pleasant as it is in the movies. It wasn't pleasant at all. I always thought if I went to jail, I would write writs of Habeas Corpus and work on my fellow inmates' appeals in exchange for contraband and all the comforts of home. Maybe I would learn a new career—like tattooing. I would be a kingpin in prison. I could even advise the guards on their divorces and custody cases. It wouldn't be that much different than now.

But in jail, I was afraid to talk to anyone. There were no guards with compassion or senses of humor. There was no cushy job waiting for me in the jail library. No Andy Dufresne to help me with my tax problems. No warm, quirky, philosophers to talk to. Mostly poor people without education or money or hygiene or teeth. You are stripped of your identity, given an orange jumper instead of your own clothes, a number instead of a name, and your opinions, your tastes, your passions, everything that makes you a human, doesn't matter.

Some people (like me) do one dumb thing and end up in jail. It's a one shot deal. Other people, when they get out, they don't learn from their mistakes. They can't find jobs, except as criminals, they can't cope, and they end up back in jail again and again.

I always had trouble taking a crap in strange places, and there was no privacy here. A stainless steel toilet in the middle of a communal cell. I recognized one of the police officers from an old case. I had cross-examined him in court. I don't remember the facts of the case, but I had made him look like he was lying. I was glad he didn't remember me. What if he took away my blanket or spat in my food?

I didn't have access to a computer or to my phone. How did I ever live without a smart phone? I couldn't even get a pencil to write with. And I had a book to write and a deadline. I guess they were afraid I would stab myself or something. A bunch of strict and arbitrary rules and guards to enforce strict and arbitrary rules.

After my arrest, my car was towed to the police impound; it was badly damaged, and the costs of being in the impound lot increased daily. Goodbye, Festiva. It was easier to let the police sell it at auction. I borrowed a car from Kendall until there would be both a criminal charge on the accident and a motor vehicle charge suspending my driver's license. I have to admit Kendall's spare car was pretty nice. A PT Cruiser. Much nicer than the Festiva. I still felt people were ridiculing me (chanting "Loser, Loser, PT Cruiser") as I drove down the road.

When I thought about that night, I realized how badly I had acted. I had gone to the party to win back Amalia, and I only made matters worse. I must say, I felt like a criminal. Which I wasn't because I had not been convicted of anything. Yet.

But the feeling was there. It's how my clients felt. These charges had serious consequences for both my driver's license and my law license. As if I wasn't already in enough trouble.

An ordinary citizen, if he has his first alcohol offense, he loses his driver's license, but, unless his job involves driving, he keeps his job. If he needs to drive to work, he can even get a red license. Like any defendant, I'd have to go to alcohol counseling, complete alcohol classes, perform community service. I'd lose my driver's license, and not only would my clients have to drive me to show houses, I'd need to find a ride to inspections, closings, and to witness interviews, meetings, and court appearances. Or I could drive on a suspended license --- like so many of my clients.

Attorneys are held to a higher standard. As a lawyer, I was obligated under the rules to self-report the conviction. That's right: the Committee can't be expected to keep track of all the drunk driving attorneys in Algonquin County.

I was required to notify the Committee of such an occurrence.

If I were convicted of an alcohol driving offense, my law license would likely be suspended, and the Disciplinary Committee would take a closer look at me. Especially in light of Judge Solomon's order.

Worst of all, I would probably be required to take another ethics seminar.

Amalia called me a few days after the accident; Kendall had called her and notified her. But something about that incident had worked because Amalia asked me out to the movies. It was hard, but I didn't tell her about the seriousness of the criminal charges. And I didn't tell her I was sorry.

We set a date for a few days later. As I worked on my cases, I fretted about the date, thinking this was my chance to make up for the way I behaved at the party and to really talk to Amalia. I arrived early at the movie house.

"I knew you weren't hurt." She sounded relieved. "It's the cherry on the ice cream. Dandelions never die." More of her quirky phrases.

There were a dozen bad movies playing in Highlands Ranch. It was my lucky night. A big blockbuster action thriller had just premiered.

"We have a lot to talk about," she said, as I purchased the tickets and we walked across the lobby to the food concessions. "I never should have invited you to the party."

"Well, what happened at the party was kind of my fault," I said, after a while.

Now this was obvious, but usually I got a little sympathy by owning up. I had so much more I wanted to say to her.

"If you want to blame someone—blame me." I paused, waiting for her to say something kind.

"I do blame you, Vanderbilt Boy," she scolded. "It was your fault, Absolutely. What were you thinking? It's your mouth again. You open your mouth and shoes fly. And I pay the broken plates. That's your problem, you don't get along with anyone. I get so furious with you, I hope the bears eat you. You're a piece of bologna. I could squish you like a cockroach."

More of her intriguing, charming, but nonsensical phrases. Maybe that's what I loved about her. Maybe that's all.

I bought her a popcorn and a Diet Coke. I knew from our marriage that if I didn't buy them before the show started, once the movie began, she would demand them, usually during the most dramatic scene. Although she said she didn't want them, I decided to go ahead and buy them anyway.

"I couldn't stand to see you with Trickey," I explained.

"Don?" she asked.

"Yes, Don," I repeated. Don. I hated the way she said it. What kind of name was Don, anyway? The most famous Donald in the world was a cartoon duck. And the most famous Ronald in the world was a clown. You don't see names like Don or Ron anymore. Kids are named Dylan or Dustin instead.

"He's just someone I know from work," she remarked.

Whew! That was a relief. It made what I said next much easier.

"I'd like to get back together."

She gave a little nervous laugh. "Back together? Who—us? Why?"

"Maybe give adoption another try?"

"I am through with lawyers," she said. "I will always love you, but…"

Here was the *but*. Go figure; she said she would always love me when she was finally through with me. She explained it with a tone of excitement. She had a job opportunity to manage an entire title company office. That was what Trickey had come to talk to her about at the party. They needed a Spanish bilingual title company manager—in Mesa, Arizona.

Hard to believe, this was good news: she wasn't interested in Trickey, but she was moving to Arizona.

Relocating for what—$20 an hour! She was excited; it was a new start for her, for her career. And there was more. She wanted me to list her house and put it on the market.

"If you don't want to, that's fine," she said. "I know a broker at Remart."

A broker at Remart. I didn't know which was worse: the idea of her moving away or the idea of her listing her house with someone else. The mental image of a gaudy blue and red Remart for sale sign in the front lawn of the Three Lakes house, it was more than I could bear.

"No, no, I'd be happy to help you," I said. "Thanks."

As we walked toward the theater where our film was playing, she dropped her bucket of popcorn in the lobby. The bucket fell face down and popcorn spilled all over the floor. She got down on her hands and knees and frantically scooped it up with her hands, pouring it back into the tub. The theater had a Hollywood motif— the carpet was posh and red—and the scattered little kernels of popcorn stared out at us.

"Carajo! Bush!"

The movie was starting, theater doors were closing, people were racing through the lobby, stepping around the mess, and she was still darting around on the floor, picking up the popcorn. I laughed, and once I started laughing, I couldn't stop. I laughed about Trickey and my car and about Amalia's relocation. I laughed about being (arguably) a criminal and about my predicament with Judge Solomon.

And mostly I laughed at watching my beautiful ex-wife, all dressed up, on her hands and knees, picking the popcorn off the lobby floor. She was tidying it up, but it looked like she was scooping it up and pouring it back onto the tub so she could still eat it.

I laughed so this was somehow my fault. You'd think this was the worst thing that ever happened to her. We saw the movie, sure, but she didn't talk for the rest of the evening.

45

When I was young, going out with women was fun. There was the excitement of flirting with them, wooing them, and ultimately seducing or being seduced by them. When it ceased to be fun or exciting, I moved on. Until the popcorn incident, I hadn't thought of ever really being single again. Of dating again.

I had stayed with Amalia for a long time. When she was young, she had trusted me to build a life with her. She had loved me, this I knew for sure. Why *me*? And how could I lose her? I could fret and fuss over what I was losing.

As we grow older, we realize that everything needs to be planned, and while we can't guarantee a result, we need to plan for contingencies. By then, it is too late to plan. I never thought Amalia would leave me. It never even occurred to me that she was so unhappy.

Maybe I would be better off without Amalia. She was like a Dyson vacuum cleaner, sexy and sophisticated, but in the end sucking the money and life and soul out of me. Maybe I would have been better off with a catalog bride from a more subservient country, not a Snow Leopard like Amalia.

I thought about the women that I knew. Several of my Xs were still available, or more correctly, I surmised, available once again. One was now a lawyer for the Post Office. Still single. Then there was the hot Southern Belle from my divorce case, the orange-haired clerk in Division W. I wondered about an old girlfriend from college. I had thought of her from time to time.

My quivering hands unbuttoning her bra beneath a blanket at an outdoor rock concert. And in a tiny dorm room. Promises made, believed, and ultimately broken. When love was mysterious and new; and whether true or not, God was alive and secretly watching; and every thought, every taste, every touch mattered.

If that had worked out I probably never would have married Amalia. I remembered her as young and sweet. A few days later, I internetted this old girlfriend on Facebook. People can't just disappear anymore, and she was pretty easy to find. I knew it was her because I saw her photo.

On her Facebook profile, she explained her career as a women's studies professor in Champaign, Illinois. What did that mean, women's studies? If it's the study of women, sign me up.

Maybe I could get a job teaching men's studies. It only seemed fair. Courses on Monday Night Football, The Hef, Howard Stern, and the Fundamentals of Beer. Another semester on Successful War Strategies, Planes, Trains, and Automobiles and a final exam on Charlie Sheen.

Hard to believe, she was still single. I read further; she had gone through at least one divorce. There was a photo of her with some girlfriends at a timeshare in Bermuda. Another photo of her shaking hands with the dean and accepting some award.

She still looked good. In the photos, she looked happy. In fact, after all these years, she looked the same. I was tempted to contact her. A simple email. Sent immediately with the press of a button. If we met again, would we be young again, like we were starting over?

How would it be, after a few weeks of emails, flying her out for a visit for a weekend, meeting her at the airport at the terminal gate? Would she say in her sweet, innocent way that it was fate? Taking her out for an expensive dinner at the Golden Corral buffet. Trying to explain why I didn't own a Subaru or a house or a 401k.

Talking about friends from college until we were bored. Checking into a hotel room I couldn't afford. Would it be the same? If it didn't last then—when we had our lives in common— how could it last now, much less even start?

After all those silences at dinner, those meaningless stories and jokes that weren't funny, all that foreplay and anticipation, making love for a full three minutes, how's that for an encore? Even if I performed magnificently, what was the point?

46

Cora asked me to come to her apartment for an appointment. She asked me in between taking lunch orders at The Overtime. I had no idea what the case was about or how much time would be involved.

"Can't we meet here at the bar?" I inquired.

"I don't want Kendall to know my business," she said. "How much do you charge?"

Charging Cora, I paused. I hadn't even thought about charging her yet. A waitress and a single mom. Whatever I could get from her in a retainer, I would have to make it last throughout the case.

"Don't worry about that," I said. "The first consultation is free. We'll talk about it when we meet."

We set the appointment for seven, and she smiled at me throughout the day as I watched her wait on tables. I wondered what the case with Cora was about. A custody matter, probably. Or a bankruptcy. Or sexual harassment.

I imagined a pretty good case against Kendall and The Overtime for sexual harassment and a hostile work environment.

Kendall had had a relentless appetite for the waitresses there. If that was the case, I would be conflicted out from representing Cora. I already represented Kendall in his divorce, and because we had an attorney-client relationship, I couldn't represent Cora against Kendall.

If anything, I would represent Kendall against Cora. Although I would feel bad cross-examining Cora, that is the job. I would recommend opposing counsel for her to interview. Good ones, but ones that were reasonable in price, and not impossible to deal with.

I had to admit, she would have a hard time finding someone she could afford as good as me.

I figured the meeting at Cora's would be short, an easy discussion on sexual harassment and why I couldn't get involved. She lived in an apartment on the north side of town on a block of ranch-style boxes rushed to construction for the vets near a military base after World War II.

At the time, it was called the American Dream. I know it seems silly now, and that dream had died out years ago.

Around six-thirty, I drove past the pot shops and porn shops, the tattoo parlors, a health food restaurant, and a gym, businesses I had no use for.

The military base had since been closed and converted into a luxury home and retail development. The houses right around the redevelopment remained cramped and run down, with structural problems. Most of the yards were dead, many of the houses were empty or in foreclosure, the homes ugly, with peeling brick or flaking asbestos siding.

Her apartment was sad, reminded me of my first my apartment off campus back in college. The walls were painted white to cover up the mold; there was a musty smell; the cabinets were old. First thing I noticed in the kitchen, there was no dishwasher.

Still, she had decorated the kitchen with wallpaper with the little red hearts and made it nice. Little refrigerator magnets—words made into poems—spread across the refrigerator door. There was a lone box of Cocoa Puffs sitting on the counter. She offered me a beer, which I declined for professional reasons. I did accept a glass of water.

"I've got a lease I need you to review." She directed me to the kitchen table. "My old landlord kept my security deposit. At least I think he kept it. He promised to mail it to me but I haven't heard from him."

Right to business. I liked that. I sat my briefcase on the floor and pulled out a spiral notebook and a pen. Why waste time on small talk, especially since I saw Cora practically every day?

"How much was the deposit?" I inquired.

"$600."

A low-end case. I knew it. It was a case based on principle. A case like this was not worth going to trial. My fees alone would make the case impractical. You need to have a case of fifty or sixty thousand dollars to be worth hiring a lawyer. And the landlords know this. That's why they keep the deposits.

"When was your final walk-thru?"

"It's been a couple of months."

"You never received an accounting of the security deposit?"

"Nope."

She was surprisingly organized. She kept her lease,

correspondence, and receipts for repairs in a manila folder in a drawer in the kitchen. She had drawn flowers on the front of the folder.

As I reviewed her lease, I took notes. The lease was only six pages long, which had been downloaded from the internet. It didn't have many of the clauses I would have included, which was good for Cora. The longer the lease from a landlord, the more loopholes.

She'd lived in the property for two years. She was never late on the rent, but she finally left because the landlord refused to make repairs.

"He was creepy. Always coming on to me. If I asked him to make repairs, he pretended he wasn't the landlord. He made fake phone calls to himself. If a repair was needed, he would say he had to talk to the landlord and walk out to his car. I would watch him from the window. He'd pretend to make a phone call, and report back, claiming the landlord was unwilling to make any repairs."

"Sounds like a typical landlord," I said. "He does that because he thinks he can avoid liability."

"And he's a *criminal*," she stressed the word. "He's got a felony on his record. I did a criminal records check on him on the internet."

I was proud of her for doing all this research. But one thing — the landlord being a convicted felon — doesn't make the case. It's a mistake to stress it. Just because he committed other crimes doesn't mean he is wrong here. In fact, under the Rules of Civil Procedure, only felonies less than five years old are admissible, except for crimes of dishonesty, and even then they go to credibility, not the hard facts of the case.

"It doesn't matter if he's a felon," I explained. "He could be a creep, have a reputation as the worst slumlord in the world, and be a convicted serial killer and still be right. It's a breach of contract claim. All that matters is if he gave you proper and timely notice about what he was deducting from the deposit and whether he was justified in keeping any of it."

I explained that forfeiture clauses and penalties in a lease were usually not enforceable and that a landlord has thirty days to refund the deposit—up to sixty if it says so in the lease—to account for any deductions for repairs, normal wear and tear excepted.

"If he failed to provide an accounting," I said, "he loses the right to withhold any of the deposit. We've got to write a demand letter, and give him the chance to make this right; if he doesn't, you can sue him for attorneys fees and for treble damages. Even if he lies about giving notice, the burden of proof will be on him to show that keeping the deposit was justified. What matters is the condition you left the property in."

"What's that mean?" she asked. "Treble damages."

"Treble damages?" I replied. "Treble means triple. It means you can sue him for three times the amount."

"Why not just say triple?" she asked. She smiled at me. There was a silence. We both laughed.

"That statute says treble, that's why," I explained. "It's usually better to use the precise words in the statute."

"I thought it was because you like to use fancy words," she said, still smiling.

"That, too," I said. "Thanks, I guess."

I felt myself being attracted to her. As I looked at the lease again, I felt her hand accidentally rub against my leg. My leg tingled. It seemed like she left her hand on my leg for a long time. More tingling. I felt the gentle touch of her hand on my knee. The room was silent. I don't know what came over me. I leaned over and kissed her.

What was I doing? It had been so long.

She kissed me back. My lips became intertwined with hers. Warm, soft lips, enthusiastically sucking my tongue. A sweet mouth that tasted like mint. I had not been with a woman for a long long time. I had given up. If I couldn't be with Amalia, I thought, I would be with Cora.

As we kissed, she closed her eyes.

"Yum," she said.

As we kissed some more, I could see myself slowly and methodically working her out of her clothes. Making love to her would be exciting, exploratory even, rather than a chore. Cora would be my escape. In the morning, after making love again, we would go out for crepes. I would live in this awful flat with popcorn ceilings and aluminum crank windows with this young bombshell. We would make love to the sounds of The Cure and Taylor Swift and Justin Beiber in her tiny bed in a room without closets and dine in a kitchen that smelled like mold.

Perhaps we could even have children of our own. That would really annoy Amalia. It is said that revenge is best served cold, and that's okay for Klingons; but I would serve revenge hot and sweaty, with the unbridled carnal knowledge of a woman in her twenties.

I would be the oldest dad in the Daisy scout troop. I thought about all the times I had watched Cora at The Overtime. This had been a long time coming.

47

But wait! What would this young, gifted, beautiful girl want to do with me? She had a big future; I had blown mine. I could be her teacher, but what could I teach? If we made love, could I whisper sweet Latin legal phrases in her ear?

She looked so young, her brain not yet completely formed. I thought of the records I had burned, the rest of my records probably still piled on the floor in Amalia's living room.

Cora probably had not even heard of the Rolling Stones. Or Lou Reed. Or even had seen a record player. She was like a different species. Maybe because her new electronic toys were so cool, everything else—everything old—was un-cool. Everything old like me.

Her phone was her drug of choice. Where was her substance, the definition of herself? Her respect for history? Cora's whole generation of self-made celebrities, with Facebook friends and texts and twizzlers and tumblers and tweets, her virtual world, a generation of zombies. More interested in how to communicate than in what to communicate. I swear to god, if I had a heart attack on the light rail, these children would take a selfie with me, slumped over in my seat, and tweeter their virtual friends. Instead of calling 911 and saving me, my death would be broadcast on YouTube. Twitterdedee. Twitterdedum. Self-absorbed. Oblivious. (I'm sure my mother said the same thing about me.)

I had made sexual contact with a client. She was a client because she had called me to review her lease, which I had done. The lease, Exhibit A, glared at me from the table, spread out in front of me.

I made sexual contact with a kiss. A kiss. A one-night stand, it was the same to the Disciplinary Committee. It didn't matter that she hadn't paid me to establish a lawyer-client relationship as far as the Disciplinary Rules were concerned. In my head, I saw the scowling face of Judge Solomon. I was the green old loser from the ethics seminar. The degenerate judge diddling the DA.

According to the disciplinary rules, she had five years to complain. Five years to get me in trouble. And despite her piercings, her sweet smell, and the warm, passionate way she kissed, she was practically a child.

I had seen the edge of the abyss. I had climbed down, eaten grubs and berries. I had camped out, gathered firewood, built a cabin there. Now it's my home, I live there. I deserve whatever happens to me. I thought about Cora and whether I could ever return to The Overtime.

I stopped before this went too far.

"Back to work," I said, breaking away. I couldn't believe I was saying this. She looked surprised. Tears in her eyes, she excused herself and walked out of the kitchen. When I was young, I lived as though there were no rules, and all I thought about was sex and making love; now rules were all there was.

I studied the lease. I would get her full security deposit from her old landlord plus treble damages. I would work for free and we would never mention this.

48

It was now summer, and almost a year had passed since the order. The drought conditions for summer were announced, watering was banned, and the pretty lawns in the suburbs grew brown from neglect.

I worried about the DUI charge, and I agonized about the book deadline. I had been given a year to write a lousy sixty-five thousand word book, and now that year was almost gone. Wasted, I scolded myself. On what? Pining over Amalia. Flirting with Cora. Litigating a bunch of low-end cases with people who ran up attorneys' fees bills they would never pay. And now I could lose my license if I failed to satisfy the judge's order. I could be disbarred, and if you are disbarred, you lose your license for eight years! At a minimum. After eight years, I would have to apply to the bar again, and prove I was rehabilitated.

It's always a good idea—when doing a new project to confer with other attorneys for advice. Every type of law has subtleties and nuances, and every court also has nuances. You can only learn these by experience.

I checked on the internet for some of my friends from law school. I hadn't kept up with anyone. Many had never even practiced law or moved out of state. Most, no doubt, were assimilated into quiet lives in the suburbs of some medium-sized city. A quiet, gentrified life like mine.

I thought it was odd that having gone to a law school at night for four years, I rarely, if ever, saw anyone from my law school class at court, at mediations or depositions, or even at the educational seminars. A third of the class dropped out first year.

One of my distinguished colleagues got kicked out after the second year. You had to have a 2.0 grade average. His was a 1.9999. A rule is a rule. A few never even passed the bar, which is only offered twice a year. Another took it twice a year for seven years until he finally passed, garnering the minimum passing score. A pass is a pass.

Several were dead already, from car crashes or cancer, mourned by their kids and their wives. One had been disbarred just after law school for growing marijuana and selling it to his clients. Go figure. His timing couldn't have been better. By the time he got his license back, marijuana had become legalized. He became the state's foremost marijuana attorney: rich, successful, even teaching the ethics course at our old law school.

I found an article from the newspaper online about one of my law school friends who had done quite well. He had had extraordinary luck. The telecommunications company where he worked had paid for his entire law school tuition, books, and fees; upon graduation, he was given a big promotion and made a regional vice president.

The company merged, then went public; he got a golden parachute worth several million dollars in stock. He dumped the stock before the market crashed and took his small fortune to start a successful financial advisory firm. He lived in a big overpriced tract house on a small lot in the high-end suburban sprawl where he had a wife and a couple of young children.

Every year he hosted a big fundraising event at an upscale hotel, and after several guest speakers and fundraising activities, he awarded himself the great and prestigious honor of being named Man of the Year. Four years in a row.

You would think I would be jealous of someone like this. He had had the same, if not fewer, opportunities as I had, with considerable more financial success. He was a good ten years younger than me. But someone has to be rich. And someone has to be happy. It might as well be him. I was still waiting for that one windfall case. As for happiness, that is another matter altogether.

49

I found his phone number online, and after several attempts and arguments with his secretary, I finally connected with him. I immediately recognized his voice.

"Darwyn VanWye," I said. "From law school."

Of course, he remembered me; I sat behind him in class for four years. Copied notes off of his laptop, exchanged briefs for minor editing, attended study sessions; we even studied for the bar together.

He seemed glad to hear from me. "Wyn," he said. "I wondered what happened to you. Hadn't seen your ads in a while."

We talked about people we had known in law school and what they were doing now. He asked about Amalia, he remembered her as well. I didn't know how to explain my troubled relationship with Amalia; I told him she was fine.

No doubt, I was a reminder of a harsher time. When our futures were fragile and inexplicably intertwined. Like we were lost war buddies. Memories of Constitutional law classes and moot court. And while there was no math in law school, there was the Rule against Perpetuities. Law school was transformative. Once you learn to think like a lawyer, you can't 'un-think' like a lawyer.

I explained that I was writing a book about the dignity and integrity of the legal system. I didn't tell him about the court's order. He wished me well, but he couldn't help me with ideas for the book. After all those courses on the rules of evidence, training to become a litigator, and hours and hours of trial practice, he had never once set foot in a courtroom.

He could advise me on a contact for an excellent ghost writer, if I were so inclined. Why hadn't I thought of that earlier? Or for self-publishing the book. He had hired a ghost writer to write his own memoir, published it on the internet. When he launched the book, he sent out announcements in the newspaper, and set up several book signings at Barnes & Noble.

Before each signing, he instructed his wife to buy dozens of copies of his book in small purchases over a week or two so he could be recognized as a best-selling author. Once he was a local bestseller, of course, book sales took off.

"I've still got boxes of these books in my garage," he offered, "if you want a copy."

"Sure," I said.

"I'll send you two or three. I'll even autograph them. I'd like to clear them out of the garage. What's your shirt size?"

"Shirt size?"

"I silkscreened some T-shirts to promote the book. I've got boxes of those, too."

"XX," I said. "Like the beer."

"What about coffee mugs? Pot holders? Ice scrapers?"

Although I didn't cook, it was hard for me to say No.

"I could always use a pot holder," I said.

"Great. I'll throw all this stuff in a box for you. I'm glad you called, I'd like to pick your brain."

"About what?" I asked.

"About my future. I'm thinking about forming an exploratory committee and making a run for public office. For governor. What do you think?"

As I remembered him, he was a likeable guy with a beautiful silky voice who got along with everyone. I had liked him. From his Facebook page, he still had his hair, he was athletically built, and he had good teeth. He had a picture perfect life and a cute, photogenic family. I didn't know his favorite color but he was an exceptional candidate.

He was, after all, a best-selling author, and Man of the Year four times in a row.

My future was clear. He needed me to help, if not manage, his campaign. If he ran for governor, I would abandon all of my other important projects and work on his election.

"I'd vote for you," I paused, as if considering. "Shit, I'd even go door to door and hand out flyers."

"You would? Why?"

I paused for a moment.

This was a test, and I was not prepared. I always did well on tests, always looked good on paper. I had to give him the right answer, not only so he would run, but so that he would hire me, maybe even appoint me to his cabinet. I could see myself as head of the Water Board, for example, or the Driver's License Bureau.

That might solve the problems with my driver's license.

"You can't be worse than the jerk-off in office now. You might as well go for it."

"Thanks, Wyn," he said. "I appreciate your support." He already sounded like he was running.

50

I made an appointment with one of the most famous and successful attorneys in town. A renown wee-wee and trial lawyer, noted for successfully acquitting several child molesters, kidnappers, and serial killers. I guess as a last resort. I still had not figured out why I was ordered to write the book. I thought about the hearing and what the judge had said. The punishment was unfair, but without the reasons behind the order, it was also puzzling.

The lawyer had been a prosecutor just out of law school, then switched sides to became a prominent defense attorney. He had won some high profile cases and several significant appeals. I thought his insight would be helpful. Aside from being an adjunct professor of law, he maintained a private practice—and a law office downtown.

When I contacted his office, his secretary informed me his schedule was filled for the next three months. After one of his big cases settled, the secretary called me back and set up an appointment.

I paced around the HUD house, anticipating this meeting. I should have had a fresh set of eyes on this case when Judge

Solomon first came down with his crazy ruling.

The day of the appointment, I gathered up my notes I had written for the book and went down to his office, which was in the downtown skyscraper where I had taken the Ethics seminar.

He must have been a very good lawyer, because his section of the building had a waterfall in the lobby. I sat in the reception area—he had really comfortable chairs—making more notes for the book, reading political cartoons in old magazines, and watching the goldfish swim around in his office aquarium.

The reception area had a view overlooking the congested boulevards and high-rises and revamped shopping malls of downtown. The magazines were over a year old. If he was such a successful lawyer, I wondered why he couldn't afford newer magazines.

After a while, his secretary ushered me into his private office with a nice cherry desk and bookshelves, wooden filing cabinets, his own secretary station, and potted plants. He was like a television lawyer, older, calmer, his glasses resting comfortably across his nose. He wore an expensive suit, and he had once been handsome. He had a beautiful, resonating voice. I told him my story, explained the situation with the order.

"That order doesn't sound right," he said. He spoke slowly, confidently, as if he was used to people paying him large sums of money so other people would mark every single word. "I went to law school with Judge Solomon. Carl and I used to play tennis together."

He made a serving gesture with his arm. Yes, Judge Solomon had a first name...

"His years on the bench must have gone to his head," he went on. "The order sounds unconstitutionally vague. Arbitrary and

214

capricious. You should have called me sooner. I could have beaten this." He paused.

"Have you considered filing an appeal? Give me a $7,500 retainer and I will look into it."

"But the time limits have passed," I said. "Months ago."

He stopped for a moment and studied his calendar, flipping through the pages of his big day timer, counting the days on his fingers. "I guess you're right," he said. "I guess there's nothing we can do."

He paused again.

"My paralegal says you also wanted to know the why of the order."

"Yes," I said. "If you have an opinion."

"I'm not sure what difference it makes, the why. You still have to comply with the order. I wasn't at the hearing, and I haven't reviewed the transcript."

"We know the who, the what, the when, and the how," he continued, as if thinking out loud. "I don't know why judges rule the way they rule. That's one of the great mysteries of the legal profession. Maybe Judge Solomon had tennis elbow the day he made the ruling. The why is because the judge said so, that's how I see it."

He looked back down at the files on his desk. "What's interesting," he said, after a while, "I'm writing a book, too."

"No surprise there," I said.

I thought about the interesting and complex legal issues he must have handled, the celebrity clients—rock stars in copyright infringement cases, sports stars and politicians in drug or sex scandals—the briefs he wrote, the arguments he made, the formidable opponents he defeated.

"About the big cases you won?" I asked.

"No," he answered. "I really should, though."

"About evolving theories of law?"

"No," he said. "But that's an excellent suggestion; I do have some interesting theories."

"About term limits for judges?"

"That's an idea worth exploring."

"About the social and philosophical impact of recent significant court rulings?"

"No, great idea, though." He paused. "The book is about my experiences kayaking. I like to get away from the legal system once in a while."

A week later I received a bill from his paralegal for $1,100 along with a detailed invoice. It included his time preparing to meet with me as a senior partner, his meeting with me, drafting his memo after the meeting, and conferring with his junior partner and an associate. I noticed it was on the invoice: when he reviewed my case, he chose the flounder for lunch.

51

Just as I began to write the book, I received a jury summons. The jury roster is based on voter registration. As long as you voted in the most recent election, you are at risk for jury duty. It was as if I was being punished for voting not to retain Judge Solomon.

Despite the fact I had other important business, I reported dutifully at 8 A.M. on the appointed day to the jury assembly room, Algonquin District Court. All the people in the room were texting or talking on their phones or reading books on their Kindles, waiting for instructions from the jury commissioner. We waited and waited. All morning.

A clerk handed me a clipboard and a pen and I filled out a jury questionnaire. This questionnaire would be read by the judge and the attorneys when the jury commissioner decided which trial to assign us to that day.

The form included questions about my background, education, college, job, etc., and previous involvement in the court system. This was a way to weed out jurors for cause, people who had relationships with some aspect of the case, the elderly or their caretakers, the E.R. docs, as well as felons, foreigners, and other such undesirables. Not that a foreigner can't sit on a jury, but if the juror couldn't understand English, the trial would go smoother without him. Finally the clerk called about thirty of us, made us stand in a line like we were back in elementary school. She led us to an elevator, and up to the courtroom.

In the courtroom, the judge greeted us and congratulated us — for our patriotism and sacrifice — in being randomly called as jurors. He introduced us to four attorneys — two for the plaintiff, two for the defendant — and congratulated us again for wasting our time. After some important conferencing at the bench, and a recitation of the parties and witnesses again to check for conflicts, one attorney from each side proceeded to voir dire; to question us and narrow us down to six jurors and one alternate. Each side got three preemptory challenges, which means they can kick you off the jury without a reason, and as the jurors were dismissed with or without cause, additional potential jurors were motioned to sit in the jury box.

You would think a prominent attorney like me would be able to get out of jury duty. The easiest way to get out of jury duty is to duck to the back of the line. Yes, the potential jurors are assigned numbers, but lawyers are notoriously bad at math, and if you don't make it into the jury box, you are not likely to be called. If you are unfortunate enough to be in the jury box, the best way to get out of jury duty is to appear to be biased in answering the lawyer's questions, siding with one side or another, or to claim hardship. Or be too educated.

A jury is supposed to only consider the evidence the lawyers present as allowed by the court, and none other. And a jury is supposed to apply only the jury instructions dictated by the judge.

I wasn't really worried. If I were a lawyer on the case, I wouldn't want me on the jury. The last thing you want on a jury is some lawyer's independent expertise, input, or opinion. You can't have intelligent, independent, engaged, thoughtful, and educated people on a jury.

The trick to picking a jury is to find strangers who will be sympathetic to your cause. The jury questionnaires and the demeanor of the prospective jurors during voir dire is all you have to work with.

I suppose that's why I was stuck on this jury. A real estate case. The questions on voir dire had to do with my experiences buying or selling a home. After about an hour of ridiculous questions by the attorneys, the jury was chosen. The identity of the alternate was withheld by the judge, though I knew. The alternate was in seat number seven. That's how the alternate is chosen. I was juror number five. My seat was fifth, the second seat on the second row.

The rest of the jury didn't know which one of them would not be able to deliberate on the case after the closing arguments. Here I was with these other losers—a nursing student, two retired teachers, a welder, a bank clerk, and an unemployed construction worker, all fine and friendly people who were cognitively incapable of getting out of jury duty.

52

Trials are won at voir dire (during jury selection) or after opening argument. The jury makes its decision not on the evidence but on whether it likes you or your client. His hair. His teeth. The coolness factor. The same way people decide elections.

By the end of opening statements, the attorneys have made their impressions, for better or for worse. The jury has been given the basic facts and arguments, and the jurors have pretty much decided the case. The rest of the trial is usually just going through the motions.

The whole trial was a waste of time. I know I was instructed by the judge to listen to the testimony of the witnesses and consider the evidence, but I had all these distractions: my own cases, finding a house for Bryan and Shauna. Measuring, photographing, and staging the Three Lakes house for Amalia to put on the market. Writing a demand letter for Cora who refused to serve me at The Overtime since I had that appointment at her apartment.

I thought about my DUI case; I worried about the book deadline. I could get the discovery, review the charges, and file motions in the criminal case. I could delay the case until the DA's caseload was piled up to the ceiling. But I couldn't stop the clock on Judge Solomon's order.

Here are the facts from what I gathered so far: a family purchased a home with a twenty-five-year-old roof, and several years later realized the roof was leaking. The former owner of the home, a widower who was so poor he could no longer afford to live in his home, sold his home to pay for medical care, and had moved to his son's basement.

The buyer's attorney claimed the seller had failed to disclose the leaky roof. The seller had written in his disclosures that the roof was only five-years-old; because of his age, his slight touch of Alzheimer's, and his wavering handwriting, he had written five years instead of twenty-five on the disclosure form when he listed the property for sale.

This was clearly a typo, as the defense attorney claimed. It was an unfortunate misunderstanding. The buyer had had the home inspected by a professional home inspector, but the week of the inspection, it had snowed, and the roof inspection was delayed. After the snow melted on the roof, the home inspector went out again and viewed the roof, and then informed the buyer's broker of the roof's poor condition. But the broker, trying to get a commission in the middle of winter, neglected to inform the buyer about the leaky roof.

The buyers didn't sue their broker, though, as I would have done. The broker was their friend, who had given them a delightful fruit basket at closing. There was testimony about the fine fruit basket. It had an arrangement of pineapple, pears, tangerines, strawberries and grapes, practically everyone who saw it bragged about it in their testimony.

The buyers sued the seller for fraud, among other things, for misrepresenting the age and condition of the roof and expected a huge judgment from the poor elderly seller. They had even refused to repair the leak—or to remove the mold caused by the water intrusion—making the home uninhabitable during all this time in order to preserve the evidence.

I observed the lawyers and some of the witnesses who sat in the courtroom. In my cases, I usually sequester the witnesses, making them wait out in the hallway so they can't be influenced by the other witnesses' testimony. And so they will be totally bored. That will teach them to testify against my client.

None of these fine advocates even requested that. I glanced back at the neon red numbers of the digital clock above the courtroom door. The testimony of each witness seemed to drag on and on.

It wasn't a case I would have even brought in front of a jury. I would have asked for a bench trial. No one was seriously injured, scarred, or maimed, and there was no one to cry for. Just a dispute over a real estate deal.

A jury doesn't want to waste its time pouring over jury instructions over percentages for comparative negligence.

I must say, as I sat in the jury box and listened to the evidence, the case was so frivolous, not even I would have taken it. What I would have guessed would be at most a two-hour hearing went on for four miserable days.

Why this roof problem was the seller's fault was mystifying. While the seller claimed the roof was fine at the time of sale, the point was clear, the buyer had inspected the home and his realtor knew about the problem. Under the terms of the contract, the buyer accepted the condition of the home.

The judge—we found on Google—had been recently

appointed. This was his first jury trial. He had been a transaction attorney with a big firm before ascending to the bench, which is why I didn't know him. The jury loved and respected him, especially when he complimented us again and again on our magnanimous and selfless acts of patriotism in not being able to get off jury duty.

The attorneys on both sides needed a little help with their objections. None of the attorneys knew the rules of evidence, and they tossed out multiple petty objections, hoping one of them would stick.

As I watched the trial, I felt myself wanting to participate. More than once, I was tempted to stand up in the jury box in the middle of the trial, shout out, and correct the attorney's objections.

As the trial progressed, the judge's evidentiary ruling were often just plain wrong. It seemed like he either didn't understand the objection or went out of his way to complicate what should have been an easy decision.

The judge wanted to appear to be fair, especially with his first jury trial—to give both sides an opportunity to properly try and present their case. Sometimes the judge seemed to favor the plaintiff; other times he seemed to favor the defendant.

Again, I wanted to interrupt. I felt like standing up in the jury box and correcting the judge's rulings.

In fact, one time the judge's ruling was so off-based, I could hardly contain myself. I felt myself stand up to correct the court. Of course, this could result in a mistrial and in all sorts of problems for me, and I should know better. But I couldn't stop myself. As I stood up to open my mouth, the judge noticed me.

"It looks like the jurors are getting restless," he said. "Time for a fifteen-minute recess."

By then I lost interest in helping the case along.

There was a pilot program where—after each witness completed his testimony—the jurors were allowed to ask questions. The jurors wrote the questions down in their juror notebooks, and the foreman, the nurse, handed the questions to the clerk. The clerk handed them to the judge.

The judge reviewed the stacks of crumpled-up paper, organized them into piles, and called up the attorneys to the bench for a sidebar. The judge and the attorneys whispered for several minutes, and the judge determined which questions were relevant and acceptable to ask of the witness. Then the judge read the jurors' question to the witness.

"And remember, ladies and gentleman of the jury," the judge instructed us, explaining the procedure, "there are no dumb questions."

The nursing student, excited about volunteering to be jury foreman, took pages and pages of notes during the testimony of each witness, googled legal terms and witness backgrounds on her phone, and wrote down dozens of ridiculous questions.

When can I fucking go home? That was my first question.

I was afraid to ask it. All I wanted to do was go to my warm and welcoming HUD home. Four days of two teams of lawyers— we checked out their qualifications on the internet, too— interrupting each other, trying to impress us with trick questions to witnesses, attacking and objecting to each other, arguing with the judge and with witnesses.

There was an expert who testified that under the laws of gravity, based on his knowledge, training, experience, and education as a professional engineer, water flows downward, causing damage from the leaky roof to the interior of the home.

This was an amazing fact that astounded several of the jurors.

The jurors wanted to give the plaintiffs some relief. Their photos and charts of their damages were convincing. Besides, the plaintiffs had several small children; they sure could use the money.

The jurors liked the graceful and confident way the plaintiff's attorney walked. Worse, one of the defendant's lawyers was missing a button on his sleeve, his tie was crooked, and he had a slight lisp. That settled the matter. Who could trust an attorney with a lisp and a crooked tie?

By unanimous decision, after considering the opening and closing arguments, the photos and expert reports, tedious, repetitive testimony and cross examinations, nitpicking objections, and going over the jury instructions, we, the jury, awarded the plaintiffs a damages award of one dollar.

53

Melanie was furious at the way the HOA was managed and the way she was treated. Members of the board still ignored her, and she had always paid her monthly dues on time. Yes, she had repainted her house without the board's prior approval; but the president of the association's house was an eyesore. Run-down, the paint flaking and peeling, the board ignored her complaints. She became almost paralyzed, lost focus at her work, and was skipped over for a promotion and pay raise. She began to look into the carryings-on of the homeowner's association.

An HOA is like junior high school. If you're not in the cool kids' crowd at the lunch table, you are either shunned or mistreated. The handful who ran the HOA changed the rules every few months. Gave themselves preferential treatment.

If the trash pick-up was Wednesday night at 7 and you placed your garbage at the curb at 6:58, you got a ticket and a fine. One month you were required to have a blue front door. The next month a red one. More fines if you didn't comply. There hadn't been a proper election in years, for lack of a quorum, and membership on the Board was by the invitation only of the Board.

When the greenbelt and the other community areas needed

maintenance or repairs, the Board went through a secretive yet complex process of soliciting bids from the least qualified contractors possible but who were related to someone on the Board. Curiously, employing the newest accounting methods, after receiving the bid, they doubled it or tripled it. The monthly dues were frequently increased; my client's requests for financial information and copies of the contracts with the association manager were always denied. At the next monthly HOA meeting—which took place at the clubhouse—Melanie sat quietly at the meeting.

When her turn came, she complained about the board and the management of the association.

After the meeting, the president of the HOA followed her out to her car, upset with her remarks. As he approached her in the parking lot, she walked away from him, which made him even madder. He grabbed her arm, she pulled away; he grabbed her again, bruising her wrist.

There were several neighbors as witnesses, including the vice president and treasurer of the Association. She called the police and had him arrested. While they investigated the criminal case, I got her an expedited hearing on a restraining order and a civil claim for outrageous conduct. Melanie appeared in court with her witnesses, who, following my advice, she had brought to the meeting; and the Board appeared for the emergency hearing.

Judge Frost, again. Just my luck.

At the hearing, people who sided with the president of the HOA sat on one side of the courtroom; people who sided with Melanie sat on the other side. The HOA went first.

The president of the Association testified that Melanie was the neighborhood nut and that the bruising incident never happened.

The vice president of the Association testified that Melanie was the neighborhood nut and the bruising incident never happened. The treasurer of the Association testified that Melanie was the neighborhood nut and that the bruising incident never happened.

The first thing I noticed: the judge played video games on his computer behind the bench during the hearing. The screen was tilted slightly so I could see the edge of the screen.

I think the game was World of Warcraft.

When Melanie showed photos of her bruised wrist and cried on the stand, the Honorable Judge Frost looked up from his video game. He appeared to believe her. When she finished testifying, the people on her side of the courtroom cheered.

It was a tough case; he said, she said. It could go either way.

"Order, order," Judge Frost said, slamming his gavel. He paused while the courtroom calmed down. He was ready to make his ruling. "I've heard the testimony of the witnesses, the arguments of counsel. I have reviewed the relevant statutes and case law, and I have weighed the credibility of the witnesses. I find Melanie Hall to be a credible witness. I believe this incident happened."

"But," he continued, and here was the cursed but, "as sympathetic as I am, there is no reason to grant a civil protection order. The police and law enforcement have other priorities rather than concern themselves with petty disputes that can be more readily resolved through the democratic process of the Homeowners Association. If Ms. Hall—or other homeowners— are dissatisfied with the Board, the declaration for the association provides for its own democratic remedies. I believe these circumstances are very unfortunate, I am sympathetic, but it's what you get when you join a Homeowners Association."

The people on Melanie's side of the courtroom were speechless; the people who sided with the president of the association cheered.

"If that's not outrageous, what is?" I said, standing and objecting to Judge Frost's ruling. It was outrageous that the judge didn't find the president's attack outrageous. "If you disagree with the Homeowners Association, you get assaulted at the meeting?"

"Counselor," Judge Frost lifted his gavel. "That's my ruling, if you don't like it, file an appeal."

He paused. "Better yet, Counselor," he went on. "If you don't like my ruling, go put it on *Oprah*."

That's what he said, word for word.

That night, the president of the HOA spotted my client walking her dog around the neighborhood. She had groomed the dog and dressed it in a pink dress. She diligently followed her dog with an association-approved plastic bag as the little dog completed its business.

The president saw her bend down and clean up after the dog. He crept behind her with the car. Pressing on the gas, he ran his car into her and crashed into a tree on the side of the road. The impact of the car tossed her like an old football against a telephone pole. He wasn't injured, but she and the dog were crushed. She was pronounced dead on the scene. There were photos of her and the dog in the newspaper. The president of the association, through his attorney, Gary Gary, later claimed his client's foot accidentally slipped on the gas pedal. He apologized, he was sorry. It was an unfortunate misunderstanding.

Without Melanie as a witness, the criminal charges against him would be dropped. After a brief investigation into the accident, no additional charges were filed. He promised to resign from the Board.

54

I have survived the red scares of my childhood, escaped the Cold War without a scratch, lived through police actions, race riots, September 11, marathon bombings, shootings in malls and movie houses.

I survived a lifetime of eating fruit doused in pesticides, driven shoddy unsafe American-built cars, shown houses with asbestos and radon and toxic mold, had unprotected sex with women in parking lots and airports, and other dangers. I never thought of attending an HOA meeting as lethal. The poor woman was tired of being told to repaint her front door.

It wasn't that she was young or that I knew her. It wasn't that I touched myself thinking about her. It wasn't that I liked her, even. It was that nothing shocked me anymore. The sudden death of Melanie seemed like the norm.

Everyone dies, and you can die at any time. You spend your whole life knowing this but when your time comes, Oh shit! you're not ready. As if life itself owes you something. As if life owes you more time. It doesn't.

In a news interview about homeowner association reform, Judge Frost denounced the senseless violence of the president of the HOA's actions, apologized that sometimes in the court system, which is run by human beings, mistakes are made, people slip through the cracks.

Unfortunately, he explained in his statement, in this case, there were no warning signs of any danger, absolutely none, and he would favor the legislature forming a task force to study the impact of equalizing the laws that govern the HOAs or increasing the regulation of the Homeowners Associations. It was clear that by forming this task force a full investigation of this unfortunate incident would be made, reports would be written, filed, and reviewed, action would be taken.

In light of the negative publicity, and after a release of an anonymous video of the dog on YouTube, the HOA dedicated a picnic table on the greenbelt in Melanie's memory.

The picnic table had been green, to match the landscaping. After a series of notices and meetings and open debates, the HOA voted to paint the table a very pleasant shade of red — the shade of Melanie's favorite lipstick — and to install a commemorative plaque on the edge of the table.

55

I told my mother about the death of Melanie Hall. She had seen the U-tube video replayed on the television news for at least a day or two. It was a terrible situation.

"Poor girl," she remarked. "And the poor Shitz-Doodle."

I also told her about the crazy order to write a book and the sanctions. The criminal charges from my own accident and Amalia's plan to move to Mesa, Arizona. Not only had I permanently fucked up my relationship with Amalia, I had jeopardized my law license as well.

I suddenly felt sorry, not only for what I did at the party, but for making such a mess out of everything. Not just the party. But for our lives. For my life with Amalia. The cute South American girl — from the open house — I had married. She deserved so much better.

My mother thought it was a good idea—it would be interesting—to go ahead and write the book, to share my experiences in the legal system. She could read it in her book club, she explained. They could discuss it over coffee and carrot cake. She suggested I call it *Yes, Your Honor*. I had a different idea. *Fuck You, Your Honor*; yes, that would be my title.

I had to make the title my own. What I want to say to every judge who makes a crackpot ruling, falls asleep, or checks his stock quotes behind the bench during trial, sees litigants as stereotypes, rushes the trial so he can recess on time, decides a case based on anger or emotion, not on the facts, precedent, and the law of the case, is too lazy or burnt out or arrogant to correct his own mistakes, or to correct the mistakes of justice. Judges who forgot why they became judges. Judges whose legacy is "He waited to retire." "He was punctual." "He sided with the big banks." "He didn't give a damn."

These are small cases, but they are not small to these people. The bigger cases are not necessarily more interesting or insightful or complicated. They involve more dollars or longer prison sentences, that's all. The cases are small, pathetic, petty, quirky, and ugly because people are small, pathetic, petty, quirky, and ugly.

56

I should have disqualified Judge Frost from Melanie's case. A long time ago. Either he didn't follow the evidence or he routinely ruled against me and took it out on my client.

If the judge is biased, or even appears biased, you can always try and disqualify him. Also, if you want to mess with the judge, or delay the case. If you succeed, the case gets continued and the case reassigned. If you fail, you have grounds for appeal.

You need to sign an affidavit explaining what you observed. Not just the court's unfavorable rulings, but the hint or appearance of bias. An inappropriate look or comment. Order the transcript from the clerk and see what you can find.

The motion to disqualify the judge is called a Rule 97 motion. The judge will no doubt disagree with the affidavit. It accuses him of misconduct. He will deny he did anything like that. But it doesn't matter, except he may remember you in another case the next time you go in front of him.

The affidavit is presumed to be true. A judge can't challenge the facts in an affidavit, and his decision to disqualify and recuse himself is based on whether the facts you allege show bias. In practice, he will almost always dump the case. In fact, any time you can present an easy way for a judge to get off a case, he will take it.

57

As I walked through security for the final hearing for Kendall's contempt, the guard who had recognized me before frisked me, smiled at me, and nodded.

I appeared at court an hour early. I had four copies of my exhibits, and cases on precedent to hand to the judge at the beginning of the hearing. I had worked up an opening and closing, direct examination and cross examination.

The first thing I did, I checked the docket. I sat with Kendall at the defendant's table. As we waited, I looked through the exhibit books, made a few last-minute notes.

I had spoken to opposing counsel (again) about dropping the contempt proceeding.

"I need to teach your client a lesson," he had said. "I hope your client brought his toothbrush."

Kendall had gone to Canada with Henry Louis without his X's permission, it is true. What was he thinking? A unique experience with Henry Louis, a pleasant memory of Niagara Falls between a father and a son? He had no excuse, no defense. If he lost he could go jail, he would be assessed his X's attorneys fees.

When the case was called, Kendall's X and her attorney still had not appeared. The courtroom was empty except for Magistrate Peach, her clerk, Kendall and me. Magistrate Peach waited for him, each minute passing, expecting him to appear.

I noticed the wood paneling, the state flag and seal mounted behind the magistrate, the big calendar on the courtroom wall. I sat at the defendant's table and watched as Magistrate Peach conferred with her clerk and looked through files and reviewed other matters. She did not say a word. I periodically looked at the clock, clicking noisily as each minute passed. The clock was loud. After exactly twenty minutes, I stood up and politely asked the judge to dismiss the case. Motion granted.

Kendall and I cheered. We thanked Magistrate Peach; you would have thought we won the super power ball lottery.

"Quid pro crow," Kendall grinned. "Am I right? Am I right?"

"That's right," I said.

"Quid pro crow," he said again.

As we left the courtroom, Kendall's X and opposing counsel, carrying his briefcase, hurried past us in the hallway.

"What about the hearing?" he asked, out of breath.

"What about it?" I replied. "It was set for 9 and it's over. We won by default."

"Wait," he said, motioning with his hand. "Let me check with the clerk. I thought the hearing was at 9:30." He looked at his watch.

I nodded "No." The hearing was decided. I wasn't going to give him a chance to re-set the hearing.

"The judge waited twenty minutes," I said. "And defaulted you. Next time, counselor, check your calendar."

Kendall's X would not bother us about Henry Louis for a while. And best yet, his X and her attorney would pay my fees as a sanction under Rule 11, which I would inflate into thousands of dollars for wasting the Court's time.

Justice ruled!

58

I think the book should contain the best and worst cases. But the list is long. Cases with hundreds and hundreds and thousands and thousands of disenfranchised, wounded, broken people. It never ends. I don't know how people became so damaged.

I had a case where my client needed emergency surgery on her eyes because she was going blind and I asked for a continuance.

"I thought masturbation caused that." That's what the judge said in denying the motion. Word for word.

I took one case where my client's grownup son tried to become his elderly father's legal guardian to take over his finances by (falsely) claiming my client was mentally incapacitated. He was a decorated war veteran and he had a good pension the son wanted to get a hold of. The fact was he was eighty-three and had a forty-year-old girlfriend. He was buying her dinners, and the son accused him of wasting his assets. But the assets were his to waste.

I was proud of him. There he was with his hot forty-year-old. I was unable to even get a date.

The court sent an investigator to determine if my client was incapacitated. But my client, a crusty old Army Colonel, refused to meet with the investigator. The son's attorney threatened to put my client in jail.

But you have to think—not how the law is written—how it is enforced. The judge was not about to put an elderly war hero in jail. At the hearing, it was obvious the man was perfectly able to take care of himself, and the case was dismissed.

It wasn't the worst case, but it may have been the meanest.

I took a case of a man who was arrested for wandering around the neighborhood, defecating on people's porches. The prosecutor was seeking serious jail time.

My client's defense was that the excrement wasn't his ---but a stray dog's.

I filed a motion to test the excrement he allegedly left hot and steaming on the neighbor's porch. The prosecutor finally admitted the cops hadn't retained a sample, and again the case was dismissed.

This was not the worst case, but it may have been one of the dumbest.

I had a child custody case where the mother in the case refused to allow my client overnights. No reason for it, she simply didn't like her X. My client was evaluated by two experts who testified over a two day hearing that he was a perfectly fit parent whose overnights with his child should start immediately.

It took the judge three and a half years to rule on the motion. Three and half years! The child was in 4th grade when the hearing occurred, and in junior high when the father finally got overnight visitation.

In the Mighty Methodist custody case, toward the end of my cross examination, my client whispered something peculiar to me; she whispered that her husband was doing the cat. I didn't know that was even possible.

"What do you mean," I asked her, "doing the cat?"

"Ask him," my client whispered.

So I asked him if he knew the family cat.

"Of course," he answered.

"Do you have a relationship with the cat?"

"Not really; it's my daughter's."

"No, what I mean is: do you have a special relationship with the family cat?"

"What do you mean by special?"

"You know."

"That's ridiculous. Absolutely not."

"One last question," I said. "If you don't have a special relationship with the family cat, how did you get those scratch marks on your arms?"

The man's face turned red.

Judge Frost wasn't playing video games anymore.

Whether it was true or whether it was blather, it didn't matter.

As far as the court was concerned, he was dead.

The best type of cases: eminent domain. That's when the government takes your property to widen a road, for example, and pays you 'just compensation' for the value of the land you lost.

You cannot lose an eminent domain case. The worst case is that your client receives the money the government offered. Most other types of cases are all or none. Not eminent domain. And you are only fighting over money.

59

The return court date for my DUI charges, I checked in with the clerk and the prosecution. The prisoners came in, in their orange jumpsuits, escorted by guards, and sat in the courtroom. The judge called the first case. I sat in the front row of the courtroom like I did with my clients. Except this time I was the defendant.

I was thinking about Cora and her hidden piercings I would never see and my lunch I had skipped at The Overtime.

What I would say to the DA, when my case was called.

Along with Judge Solomon's order, an alcohol-related conviction would be a disaster. With a DUI conviction, I wouldn't be able to drive to court. I wouldn't be able to drive to sell real estate. And the Committee would examine me further, look into all my cases, all my dealings. Anything less, I would still have to write the book from the judge's original order, but I would likely survive it.

As I waited, I saw Traffic Jack in the courtroom. I recognized him by his fine black suit and his red silk handkerchief sticking out of his front jacket pocket. He looked older; he had lost most of his hair. I had sat down next to him as the first cases were called.

"You look familiar." He looked up from his briefcase.

"I'm a lawyer, too," I explained. "I used to run ads on television."

"No, I know you from somewhere else." Silence. He looked at me, inquisitively.

"You used to be my lawyer," I said, after a while. "A long time ago."

"Pardon me if I don't remember you. How are you?"

I told him I was writing a book about the dignity and integrity of the legal system. Naturally, he was writing a book, too, about NASCAR, the history of sports racing.

"Speaking of books," he asked. "Do you know Judge Solomon?"

"Sure," I said.

"I heard he's part of a pilot program—he's sanctioning lawyers who are behind in their child support and alimony. I heard he even ordered one lawyer to write a book. It's insane."

I smiled to myself. It all made sense to me then. The judge was right to punish me for my delinquent alimony, although I still think he was wrong about the form of punishment. After all I put myself through, it was a relief to be found wrong about Judge Solomon's order.

A lawyer has a hard time admitting he is wrong; we can always come up with some argument supporting our position. I always assume I am right and the judge will agree with me. Because I am the lawyer, and how could he not? Especially my own case. But it's one thing to know a fact, it's another to believe it. The smallest detail, the case can turn against you. All I ask is a fair opportunity to present my case and a neutral, rational decision-maker. All I ask is the opportunity for a fair decision. The fact that he was right to sanction me for the unpaid alimony made me feel better.

It is easier to make a mistake, to be wrong, rather than to be wronged. To be unfairly singled out and suffer a travesty of justice.

Some cases are just decided unfairly; even though you are noble and right, there is no chance, the door is shut and locked tight, the case is poisoned, and there is nothing you can do. It is one of those obstacles in life. You can fret and worry and agonize over it, whine about it, become the neighborhood nut, allow it to paralyze you, waste an entire year. Or you can accept it and move on, however unjust, and simply do it, write the book already.

Now all I had to do was write it. My year was almost over. The Broncos season was about to start up again.

"Good to see you, again," the lawyer went on, as his first case was called. "I'm sorry I don't remember you. I hope in whatever matter I represented you back then we won."

Traffic Jack saved a lot of drivers' licenses that day.

60

By the time the prosecutor called me up, there was only one small file remaining on the table in front of the courtroom. The DA—a young woman this time—looked about Cora's age—who can tell anymore?—dressed up in a nice suit.

She showed me her case file. There were numerous inflated charges against me. I had reviewed the elements of each charge she needed to prove, including the mens rea requirements. There were witness statements from various police officers but no actual witnesses who saw me driving.

"I must admit," she said, "you have a clean driving record."

"Sorry to disappoint you." I returned her smile.

In looking at the file, my blood test was not properly certified, and there was no forensic evidence that I drove within two hours of being intoxicated beyond the legal limit or drove on the wrong side of the road.

She wanted to pursue the case anyway, prove intoxication by the roadside sobriety test, the way it was done before blood tests and breathalyzers. There were notes in the police reports that on the night of my arrest I had slurred speech and smelled like beer.

"Let me get this straight?" I said. "You want to have the incompetent police officers who messed up the blood test testify they didn't mess up the roadside test?"

That sounded like reasonable doubt.

I could beat the case. But just as I tell my clients, when you go to court, no matter how good the facts, your chances at trial are at best fifty/fifty. Here the bungled blood test was a break, but I still had bad facts. The incriminating observations of police officers.

And I began to think in a way I hadn't thought before. The worst fact of all: I was guilty. A small matter for a lawyer usually.

I had been ordered to write a book about the dignity and integrity of the legal system. Where was *my* integrity? Wasn't I part of the legal system?

I had broken into Amalia's house and twisted the cord to her garage door opener. I had not paid Amalia's alimony. I had not satisfied the order to write the book; in fact, I tried to argue my way out of it. And I had driven under the influence. As a lawyer, I couldn't lie to the judge about the circumstances surrounding my arrest.

The DA was quiet as she looked through the case file. I was thinking about Amalia, and her relocation to Arizona. I never went with her to visit her country. I never learned her language. I loved her in my way, the only way I knew how, but I had shut her out.

I had been lucky to marry Amalia, I had blown it. I had provided for her, I had not supported her. The break-up with Amalia was my fault. Mine. I had to own it.

"Why not find some major felony to charge to me with?" I chided.

"I wish I could," the young prosecutor replied, disappointedly. "These are serious crimes. I know these are just traffic offenses, but the DA's office is fed up. They have a zero tolerance policy."

"It looks to me you don't have much evidence."

"I guess we can agree to disagree," she said.

"What does that mean, anyway?" I opined. "You can't agree to disagree. You either agree or you don't."

"It's just an expression."

"Well, it's stupid. Words have meaning. It's like saying a 'foreseeable' future. The future is at most predictable, but it's not foreseeable. It's the future."

There was a silence as she studied the case file again. The next group of defendants was beginning to filter in the courtroom.

"I'll go ahead and request a jury trial," I went on. "I have to say, I'm almost fifty-years-old. I can't afford to travel, I don't do much in the way of entertaining. Movies bore me, my wife left me, and I don't even have sex anymore. The only thing I have to look forward to—the only thing I will really enjoy—is making you prove your case."

"On minor traffic violations?"

"It's a matter of principle for me. You will have to earn your conviction. You've got to prove every element of your case beyond a reasonable doubt."

With great power comes great responsibilities; and with great egos come great insecurities. The trick is: to be a prick but not too much of a prick.

Normally, I would hold out for a better deal. I was hungry; I needed a meal.

The prosecutor offered me a plea to avoid the cost and risk of trial. She showed me a list of possible lesser charges I could plead to. Defective brakes. Defective headlights. Interfering with private property. This was the menu she offered me. None of them were alcohol-related offenses, and I tried not to smile with relief.

I still had to enter a plea. Any one of these fictions would become a legal fact if I accepted a deal, whether or not it was true, whether or not there was any basis for it whatsoever.

When I stood before the judge to allocate to my crime, the judge asked me how I pled:

"Guilty," I said.

The word stuck in my throat as I said it. I hadn't had a traffic violation on my record since I got my law license. It wasn't even a crime I had committed. I was guilty of so much more.

Justice unfurled!

I pled guilty to one count of playing with a toy car on a public street, a minor infraction. All the other charges were dismissed with prejudice.

61

This is the book I wrote. Word for word. My criminal case resolved, I barely had time to write the book to try and save my law license. After I left the courtroom, I lingered by the entrance to the courthouse behind the line for security. Lawyers, witnesses, and jurors rushed past me on their way to their trials and hearings. I pulled out my calendar and counted the days. I checked my phone and cleared my schedule. Once you learn to think like a lawyer, you can't 'un-think' like a lawyer. I had already missed the deadline for the appeal; I wouldn't miss the book deadline. The book took days, sitting at the bar at The Overtime.

Cora gave me the cold shoulder at The Overtime—until I wrote the demand letter to her old landlord, and she received a full refund of her security deposit. Then she was flirty and filled with smiles.

A full-length book, it was quite a challenge. In my law practice, I wrote letters, briefs and motions. Under the Rules, motions longer than fifteen double-spaced pages were discouraged. And when I drafted a motion, I summarized the facts, recited the law, applied the law to the facts, and came to my conclusion. With the book, I didn't know where to start. I wasted some more time, looking for tips on the internet.

I worked hard on the book, harder than any motion or legal brief. Agonizing about the book, staring at the screen on my laptop, adding and deleting, writing and re-writing, cutting and pasting, it was an exercise in self-reflection and self-loathing.

I thought about Amalia and her move to Arizona. Although I would always miss her, she had the right to move on.

The balance of my life was like a Petri dish, an ongoing experiment. You change one ingredient and the whole concoction can go wrong, and try as you might, you may never find the formula again. I had to face the fact that I lost Amalia, and she would never come back.

At first, I wrote about the system to show its lack of integrity. As I sat and wrote at the bar, I thought about everything that had happened since I got the judge's order. I looked through my notes from my file. I did my best to decipher them.

The integrity of the legal system is not pin-striped suits or law offices with fountains and potted plants. It is not the rules or case-law, courtrooms or the judge's chambers. Integrity lives in the hearts and souls of the lawyers, the judges, the prosecutors, even the witnesses and the litigants. I thought about the essay I had written when I first applied to law school. My oath when I became a lawyer to protect the people and uphold the constitution. No one ever said that would be easy.

Judge Solomon had ordered me to write a book; it was a nutty order, but the judge was right to do it. Some orders are just nutty. Your choice is to accept the order or appeal. And you can't help everyone, right every injustice. Some people simply can't be saved.

I left the title the same.

I called the Disciplinary Committee to warn them about the book. I never heard back. I guess the Committee was too busy giving seminars.

There were some typos in the book, no doubt, and some misspellings; I simply ran out of time. I wrote the book in short chapters so it would be easy to read. I gave myself an A for effort.

I was worried about the length. Technically, the word count was short, and I had not complied with the letter of the order. I couldn't imagine the judge sitting down and counting the words. The order said sixty-five-thousand words. I managed to write my book in much less. That's all the book needed, I would argue; therefore, that is all that was required.

Or I could stick a bunch of extra words back in.

I pictured Judge Solomon in his black robe as he sat in his chambers, maybe snacking, for example, on a box of Bugles, turning the little book page by page. His demeanor slowly turning into a grin. Maybe his clerk and his bailiff would also read the book. Maybe if he liked it, he would share it with the other judges.

I found out how the masses of unemployed people spend their time: in chat rooms on the internet, on Facebook and Twitter. I'm not sure if they are on the internet because they are unemployed or if they are unemployed because they spend too much time on the internet.

There were a number of blogs about writing a book. The best definition of a blog I read is this: a blog is an internet forum where a smart, intriguing, and interesting person reveals small, intimate thoughts and details about his life and immediately becomes uninteresting.

I read advice that when you write a book you shouldn't use adjectives; you shouldn't use adverbs; you shouldn't use passive verbs; you shouldn't use semi-colons; you shouldn't use exclamation points. I ignored the good advice from the fine experts on the internet about writing. If the book works, that is the only thing that matters.

The best advice about writing a book I learned from up on the Google is that when you write a story, it is better to show the story rather than tell the story. Then the writer who advises this usually goes ahead and simply tells the story.

A lot of books promoted on the internet have five star reviews. Some books have dozens of them. They must be very good books, I would say; magnificent, even spectacular, to be so universally admired.

Most lawyers who write a book assume it is good. Because they wrote it, and they are lawyers. They think their lives and stories, no matter how long-winded or dull, are inherently interesting. When I wrote my book, I naturally assumed it was bad.

There are no exciting car chase scenes or shooting scenes, no steamy sex scenes in my book, and nothing gets blown up. After a bit of self-reflection, in my totally unbiased opinion, I gave the book a rating of two stars.

And I had a reader, Judge Solomon. At least one. Guaranteed. That's more than most books have. I calculated the book took me eighty hours, sometimes writing frantically, sometimes unable to write at all. That is three hundred and twenty hours in the inflated way which lawyers charge their fees. Plus costs for designing and printing a cover, for copying, for filing the book, not to mention the legal and internet research, the travel time, and all the

Reubens at The Overtime.

As for the cover, I designed three different versions and set them out on the bar for Cora, Kendall and his hunting buddies to see. I liked the one with the goofy gavel and the splattered graphite border.

No one to bill for this project. I have to say, though, when I saw the paperback copy of the printed book, I was a little proud.

It was the year of the HUD house. The year that—once and for all—I moved on. The HUD house on Hickory Lane finally sold, the real estate market was beginning to turn. I listed Amalia's house and sold it to Mr. and Mrs. Bryan and Shauna Reading, as joint tenants with the rights of survivorship. After the third showing, sitting in the family room of the Three Lakes house, Shauna confided that they, Bear and she, (meaning Shauna) loved the "Rainbow House." Every room was painted a different color. Close to the park. Perfect for starting a family.

I received a full real estate commission. I double-ended the deal. After the closing, I went to the Three Lakes house and helped Amalia load her furniture into her Mayflower truck. I retrieved the rest of my record collection. I said goodbye to the house, and I said goodbye to Amalia. She gave me a little hug, and I kissed her on the cheek. That was the last time I would see her.

I paid Amalia her delinquent alimony so she could relocate with her job. The alimony order was a court order, after all. There was no excuse for not paying it.

I would send Amalia a Christmas calendar to her new address.

The rest of the commission to the IRS.

The day the book was due, I filed a certification of compliance with the court's order. My slate was wiped clean. As far as anyone was concerned, my punishment had never happened.

At the courthouse, I dressed in my finest pinstriped suit, fresh from the dry cleaners. As I brought the clerk a copy of the book, I saw Judge Solomon's bailiff packing law books, carrying out boxes. Budgets being what they were, he was vacating his office and taking his dilapidated old fan with him. After all that, he never would read my book, he was busy, leaving his cases behind him; he had ascended to his new appointment on the Court of Appeals.

There was a judicial vacancy opening up in the Algonquin County District Court. I inquired from the bailiff how to get an application. More details would be forthcoming in a well-respected, influential, and prestigious legal journal.

Call the deputy mayor, the lieutenant governor!

Maybe I will give it a whirl.

Did you win, Wyn?

It depends on your definition of winning. I do not own a Dairy Queen. I did not become a mailman. I even started advertising my law practice again. Sometimes losing less is winning. Sometimes surviving is. As a lawyer, I could argue either way.

All I do know is, if I ever saw Judge Solomon in a casual setting, for sentencing me to write this book, I would thank him.

ABOUT THE AUTHOR

Craig Chambers is an attorney and short story writer residing in Littleton, Colorado.

CPSIA information can be obtained
at www.ICGtesting.com
Printed in the USA
FSOW02n2325140517
34195FS